HATING THE BOSS

KRISTEN GRANATA

MORE FROM KRISTEN

Want to gain access to exclusive news & giveaways?
Sign up for my monthly newsletter!

Visit my website: https://kristengranata.com/
Instagram: https://www.instagram.com/kristen_granata/
Facebook: https://www.facebook.com/kristen.granata.16
Twitter: https://twitter.com/kristen_granata

Want to be part of my KREW?

Join Kristen's Reading Emotional Warriors
A Facebook group where we can discuss my books, books you're
reading, and where friends will remind you what a badass warrior
you are.

Love bookish shirts, mugs, & accessories?
Shop my book merch shop!

To my real-life kindergarten dream team,
Trish, Dorthy, Stacey, & Jess:
I couldn't survive what we do if I didn't have you.
Thank you for being there for me in some of
the toughest times of my life & for making me laugh
until my stomach hurts.

And to all the teachers out there,
underpaid, underappreciated, & overworked:
You guys rock! Don't ever forget how important you are.

CHAPTER ONE

Days Left Until Summer Break: 80
Jaxon

"*Yes, Jaxon. Oh, God. Yes!*"

See that woman? The one having the best orgasm of her life? That's my girl, Raegan. She's beautiful. Long, blond hair. Striking green eyes. Thick thighs. More-than-a-handful tits. She's perfect. This moment is perfect.

It's been a long time coming. Things weren't always this great. We had a bit of a rough start. I accused her of stealing my dead grandmother's ring. She swore she didn't. We waged war against each other for months.

But all that's behind us now.

"I love you, Raegan," I whisper in her ear. "I love you so much."

She cups my face, gazing into my eyes. "I love you too."

It's my turn to pump my release and when I'm done, I hold her in my arms. We're sated and relaxed. Happy. For the first time in a long time, everything feels right.

Raegan's stomach lets out a loud growl. I chuckle. "I'll get our tacos." I plant a kiss on her forehead and roll out of bed.

Life is crazy. A chance encounter can tilt your entire world on its axis. You can't always see the reason why things happen in the beginning, but eventually, it all clicks into place. Everything makes sense.

One second you're miserable, and the next you're making post-sex tacos for your girlfriend on Valentine's Day with a goofy smile plastered on your face.

I carry our plates into my bedroom, water bottles tucked under each of my elbows.

Raegan's out of bed, hunched over my open dresser drawer.

What's she looking for?

My body stills when I glance down at the blue velvet box she's clutching in her hand.

No. It can't be. "What are you doing?"

Tears well in her wide eyes. "Jax, I can explain."

The plates slam as I drop them on top of the dresser. I yank the box from her fingers and flip open the top, staring at the sparkling ring in disbelief.

See that guy? The one whose life just crumbled before his eyes? That's me, Jaxon.

Biggest chump in the fucking world.

CHAPTER TWO

Six Months Earlier ...

CHAPTER THREE

Days Left Until School Starts: 30
Raegan

*D*id you know there's an entire playlist on Spotify called *Badass Slow-Motion Walking Songs?*

Imagine that scene in a movie when a car or building explodes. Now picture the actor walking away from it in slow motion, flames roaring around him, smoke billowing into the atmosphere. He's totally unfazed by the fact that he could be hit by flying debris at any moment. Notice the song playing in the background? It's a rock song, lots of drums, and it amplifies the man's badassness as he leaves the fiery scene.

That's how I envisioned myself leaving the courthouse on the day my divorce was finalized.

I had the playlist ready to go on my phone and everything. Earbuds? *Nope.* I was going to blast that shit the whole way across the parking lot.

But when the sun hits my face as I exit the courthouse, all I want to do is cry. And take a nap. Then cry some more.

Seven years I'd been married. Might not seem long to people

who've been together for decades, but it felt like an eternity for me. I tried to make it work. I gave and I compromised. I cooked, I cleaned. I gave him a blowjob every night. *Every night.* Don't tell me I wasn't dedicated.

It didn't matter though. No matter what I did, it wasn't good enough. Didn't change the fact that I was married to an asshole. In Andrew's defense, he didn't mean to be an asshole. His father's a controlling prick, so he didn't know any different.

In the beginning, Andrew was sweet. Doting. At least, I thought he was. I was young. Turns out you don't know much about love or what you stand for when you're twenty. That's why they tell you not to get a tattoo until you're at least twenty-five. They say your brain isn't fully equipped to make long-term decisions before then. And when I say *they*, I mean the proverbial "they." You can hate them all you want, but *they* are always right.

It took me a while to realize that what I once thought was caring was actually possessive. What I thought was confidence was just condescending. Don't get me wrong, Andrew wasn't the worst person I could've been with. He didn't beat me or anything.

My mom says that's how you know something's wrong: You start downplaying your unhappiness and comparing it to domestic abuse.

Sometimes, I'd wished he would hit me. Just once. At least then I wouldn't have felt so guilty about leaving him.

That's sick. I realize that now.

Needless to say, I wanted this divorce. I'd been the one who'd asked for it. I'd reached my breaking point. Now I know why people call it that. You bend so much that you eventually break in half. Two parts: Who you once were, and the angry, resentful person you've become.

In the end, I gave him the house, the dog, my full bookcase, and all my Christmas decorations. Even my favorite sugarplum fairy ornament I'd had since I was a kid. I packed up the essentials and left everything else behind. That's how badly I wanted out. That, and the fact that I couldn't afford to fight him for any of it in court.

So how come I'm not slow-mo walking to my car right now? I should be thrilled and relieved that this is over.

I swing myself into my car, turn the key in the ignition, and crank up the air conditioning. As the stream of air cools my skin, I take a minute to scroll through my missed calls and texts.

BECCA: CONGRATS! YOU'RE A FREE WOMAN NOW!
   Mary: Congratulations! It's all over now
   Sammi: Woohoo! Moving on to brighter skies.
   Andrea: Yasss queen! Single & ready to mingle
   Kerry: Ding, dong, the dick is gone!

IT'S WEIRD THAT EVERYONE'S CONGRATULATING ME. IT'S EVEN weirder when I think back to these same friends congratulating me on my wedding day.

Should I feel proud of being a divorcee? I feel as if I'm wearing a scarlet D on my chest. Like I should run and hide before people with pitchforks try to tar and feather me in the middle of town square.

I don't think my small town in New Jersey has a town square, but still. It could happen.

I click on Becca's name and lift the phone to my ear.

"Hey! How'd everything go?"

I sigh. "It went fine. I'm just exhausted."

"I'm sure. Why don't you go home and take a nap? Then you'll be recharged for tonight."

"I don't think I'm feeling up to coming out tonight."

"Oh, no. You are not getting out of this one. You can't sit home and mope around. You need to be with your friends. Your very excited friends who got babysitters to watch their asshole children for the night."

I slump forward and rest my forehead against the steering wheel. "I don't feel like celebrating."

"Then you can sit at the bar and cry into your mojito. You're coming out."

"Fine. But it's your fault if the townspeople stone me to death."

"What? Is this another one of your book references that I don't get?"

"Never mind. I'll see you tonight."

Chucking my phone onto the seat beside my purse, I glance out the windshield just in time to catch my now ex-husband waltzing out of the courthouse.

In the year it took us to get divorced, Andrew lost a good ten pounds. I'd always tried to convince him to come running with me when we were married. *I only run if I'm being chased* was his response. Funny how he suddenly found the desire to get in shape once I was out of the picture. Bastard looks better than he did when we first met.

I, on the other hand, found the ten pounds he'd lost, and tacked on another five for good measure. I'd lost my drive and stopped working out. I envy the people who stop eating when they're stressed. I'm an emotional eater. I eat my feelings, and unfortunately, they aren't fat free. They taste a lot like Ben and Jerry's.

I peel my eyes away from the man I used to love and back out of my parking spot. Instead of leaving the courthouse to my Spotify playlist like a badass, I'm crying to Don Henley's *Sometimes Love Just Ain't Enough*.

"I AM *NOT* GOING IN THERE."

Becca tugs on my elbow. "Come on. She already spotted us."

My bottom lip juts out. "But there's balloons."

"I swear I told her not to get them. You know Kerry."

The bouncer hands my license back and jerks his thumb toward the embarrassing scene that awaits me. "Those balloons are funny."

I glare at him. "Good. You can have 'em."

"They're trying to be supportive and cheer you up," Becca says. "We just want you to be happy again."

"I know, I know." I blow out a puff of air and lift my chin. "All right. Let's get this over with."

We step inside the bar and I plaster a smile on my face. One thing my marriage taught me is how to hide my emotions from anyone and everyone. I've become so good at lying, even to myself, I could probably pass a lie detector test. I'd be a valuable asset if the CIA ever wanted me.

My friends wave excitedly, dressed to the nines with hair and makeup on point. We are the epitome of women in their thirties. It's like we're stuck in limbo: Too old to let loose the way we did in our twenties, but too young to feel content at home with a pair of knitting needles.

I cringe as I gaze up at the six shimmery gold balloons, each of them broadcasting my humiliating news to the entire bar: *I'm not with stupid anymore. Divorced AF. Ditched the dick. Unhitched. Just divorced. Legally single.*

To make matters worse, Kerry's holding a black sash. I don't know what it says yet, but I wonder if it'd be strong enough to act as a noose.

"Congrats, mama!" Kerry raises the sash above my head.

I duck out of the way. "I love you, Kerr, but I'm not putting that thing on. The balloons are more than enough."

Her cheerful expression falls. "Here." She shoves a mixed drink into my hand. "Maybe you'll change your mind after a few of these."

Mary, Andrea, and Sammi offer me smiles laced with pity.

"Oh, no," I say, waving my free hand. "Don't look at me like that. It's done and over with. Let's just forget about it."

"How did it go today?" Andrea asks.

"Quick and easy. If you ladies ever need to get divorced, the Divorce Center is the way to go."

"Good to know," Kerry says. "I'll make that the new threat I throw at Brad the next time he decides to stay out late after work."

"He's still doing that?"

"Don't wanna talk about it." Kerry raises her glass. "To Rae. Let's get you laid tonight."

I shake my head but drink to her toast anyway.

"What?" she asks. "The best way to get over someone ..."

"She just got divorced," Sammi says. "Give her some time."

"I need to lose this weight first." I gesture to my stomach. I'm wearing a flowy top, but we've all seen the bulge underneath that's currently hanging over the waistband of my jeans.

"Oh, thank God," Kerry says, wiping her forehead for effect. "I was hoping you weren't accepting this as your new physique."

Mary and Becca swat each of Kerry's arms and exclaim her name in unison.

"It's okay," I say. "We don't have to pretend like I haven't gained some weight."

"You should come kick-boxing with me," Andrea says.

"I will definitely take you up on that. We've got one month until work starts in September, and I plan on walking through the doors of Roosevelt Elementary a changed woman."

"Good for you," Becca says.

Andrea's glass slams onto the bar. "Speaking of work, did you read the board minutes?" She pulls her phone from her cleavage and scrolls through it at lightning speed. "Dr. Reynolds was let go!"

My eyes go wide. *Our principal was fired?*

"Are you serious?" Mary snatches Andrea's phone and we huddle around it to read the e-mail.

Board minutes are like gossip columns in the education world. Salaries, firings, and retire-ings are e-mailed to every employee working for the Board of Ed.

"Good riddance. I've had enough of these female principals on a power trip," Kerry says. "We need some testosterone in our school. Someone to scare all those little shits into behaving."

Sammi shakes her head. "It's going to take a lot more than a man in a suit to scare our students."

"Forget the kids," Mary says. "We need to teach parents how to discipline their children. I'm tired of getting hit, and then asked what I did to make the kid hit me."

"Amen to that."

The six of us have been friends for as long as we've been teaching at Roosevelt Elementary school. We refer to ourselves as the kindergarten dream team. Not every grade level in our building is as tight-knit as we are. Not every teacher pulls her own weight. But in our group, we're like a well-oiled machine.

You need a good support system when you're battling a room full of five-year olds. Teaching kindergarten isn't for the faint of heart.

I shudder at the thought of going back to work with my maiden name. The looks, the whispers, the questions, all from co-workers who act like they care just because they want the gossip. At least I have thirty-one more days of summer bliss.

I lean toward the bartender who's mixing a drink in front of us. "Can we have a round of shots, please?"

"What's your poison?" he asks.

"Whatever's strong enough to help me forget about these balloons hovering over my head."

He chuckles. "Got it."

Soon after we down our shots, the bartender pours us another round. "These are from those gentlemen over there."

All six of our heads swivel in the direction of the bartender's finger. Four smiling men raise their own shot glasses.

"What does this mean?" Sammi asks. "What do we do?"

Andrea pats her on the back and hands her a glass. "We do the shot, babe."

"Won't they think we'll want to sleep with them if we do the shot?"

"They're men. They already think everyone wants to sleep with them." Kerry lifts her chin and throws back the amber liquid.

I wrap my arm around Sammi's tense shoulders. "The bartender poured them right in front of us. No one's getting roofied. Now smile at the nice men and drink your free alcohol."

"They're coming over here." Kerry nudges me toward the front of our circle. "You're single now. Go get 'em, tiger."

I shoot daggers at her over my shoulder. On second thought, maybe that sash will come in handy. I could use it to strangle *her* instead of myself.

"Do that thing," Mary whispers, and the girls nod.

I scan the men as they approach. "The short one is the leader. He's the most muscular because he's overcompensating for his height. I say he's in finance. The tall, scrawny one looks like he's a doctor. He's the quiet type. The blond knows he's good-looking, but he's not a douche about it. I say he's a personal trainer."

My eyes land on the fourth man, lingering much longer than they did on his three friends. Tall, dark, and handsome doesn't quite do him justice. Thick, tousled hair. A clean-shaven, prominent jawline. Broad shoulders. He's the only one in the group wearing a suit—a suit that looks like it's tailored perfectly to his body. You know when you can just tell a guy is fit underneath his clothes? The way his shirt stretches across his chest, the tapering at the waist. Yeah, that's him.

Also unlike his friends, who are surveying each of us to figure out which one they want to hit on, this one's eyes are zeroed in on me. He walks with a confident stride, lips curved into a flirty smirk. It's the look of a man who knows what he wants. And he expects to get it.

"What about him?" Andrea asks.

"He looks like an executive of some sort. Definitely in a position of power. And judging by the fit of those pants, I'd put money on him having a fantastic ass."

The girls burst into giggles just as the men arrive.

"What are you ladies laughing about?" the short one asks. The leader always speaks first. *Point for me.*

"Oh, nothing," I say. "Inside joke."

Mr. Sexy in a Suit shoves his hands into his pockets. "How much money would you put down?"

My nose scrunches. "What?"

"You said you'd bet that I have a fantastic ass. How much would you wager on that?"

I clench my jaw to keep it from falling open. "What do you read lips?"

"I do," he says with a cocky grin.

I tap my finger against my chin as I make a show of assessing his body once more. "I'd bet fifty bucks I'm right."

"That's a confident bet."

"I'm a confident woman." *At least I* was *before seven years of marriage stifled me.*

Mary rests her elbow on my shoulder. "Fifty bucks from each of you says my girl is right about everything else she said about you too."

The men exchange glances before their pint-sized leader speaks for them. "You're on. Let's hear it."

I point to each of them. "Doctor. Finance. Personal trainer."

Their eyebrows lift as they dip into their wallets and place their cash in my hand.

Mr. Sexy in a Suit narrows his dark eyes. "And I'm just the guy with the nice ass?"

"That hasn't been proven yet," I remind him. "But I'd say you run things at your job. The boss, like a CEO or something."

A smirk tugs at his lips. "How'd you do that?"

"It's a gift. A weird gift that serves no purpose or utilizes any real talent."

"I wouldn't say that. That was pretty impressive. Do you work for the FBI?"

I lean closer to him and say, "If I told you, I'd have to kill you."

He laughs, revealing a set of perfect pearly whites. It's a stark contrast from his tan skin. I'd also like to note that his laugh is sexy. You don't realize how important a person's laugh is until you're on a date with someone whose laugh sounds like a dying mongoose.

I hold my hand out, palm facing up. "So are you going to ante up?"

"I don't have cash on me, but I'd love to buy you and your friends another round."

I pretend to mull it over. "Hmm. Not sure that'll cover your debt."

He dips down, closing the gap between us to position his lips at my ear. "I can come up with other ways to repay you."

Heat crawls up my neck and into my cheeks. This guy is used to getting his way. I'd bet girls throw themselves at him on the regular. I try to appear unaffected and hike a shoulder. "I'll take another shot of whiskey to start."

I peer up at him as the bartender takes his order. Everything about him is smooth. His skin, his voice. *Those lips.*

It's been so long since I've been kissed. I mean *really* kissed. A hands-in-the-hair, bodies wrapped around each other, all-consuming kiss.

Somewhere along the line, the desire I'd had for Andrew turned into disgust. Resentment will do that to you. It trickles into your blood like a poison, slow at first, until it's coursing through your veins. It overrides every other feeling you have, making it impossible to see through the blurriness of anger and disappointment.

I snap back to the present moment when a shot glass is handed to me. The stranger clinks his beer bottle against it and takes a long swig. His eyes flick up at the balloons. "Those for you?"

I grimace at the reminder. "Yup."

"Sorry to hear that."

"Everyone else seems to think congratulations are in order."

He shakes his head. "Divorces are sad."

"You wouldn't think so with how many couples were in the courtroom today."

"Just because it's common doesn't make it any less tragic."

He's right. His honesty puts me at ease with this conversation. Either that or the whiskey is melting my reserve.

"I feel like a failure," I confess. "Just another idiot who married the wrong person."

"You're not an idiot. Everyone makes mistakes. At least you had good enough sense to correct it. Do you know how many people stay stuck in their mistakes?"

I tilt my head to the side, turning his words over in my mind. "That actually makes me feel a little better."

"Just a little? Guess I'll have to keep trying."

My eyes bounce back and forth between his eyes, smiles tugging at both of our mouths. Flirting like this breathes some much-needed life into my lungs. *I've missed this.*

Andrea pokes her head between us. "Are you single?"

The sexy suit keeps his eyes fixed on me when he says, "I am. Wouldn't've come over here if I wasn't."

She fans herself with her glittery clutch. "Sexy and a gentleman? He's just the guy you need tonight, Rae." She winks and bounces back to our friends.

I'm about to apologize for my friend's forwardness when I realize something. Why should I apologize? Andrea is being herself. Nothing wrong with that. I'm sure this cocky man in a suit wouldn't think twice about apologizing for anything he says.

I've apologized to Andrew enough to last me a lifetime—mostly for things I didn't need to apologize for in the first place.

"So what's Rae short for?" the Sexy Suit asks.

"Raegan." I extend my hand toward him. "And you are?"

"Jaxon."

When his large hand engulfs mine, goosebumps spread up my arm. He doesn't let go right away, his coffee-colored eyes penetrating mine.

Black coffee. No cream or sugar. Just the rich, bold taste. *Wouldn't I love a sip.*

It feels like forever since I've touched a holding hand that felt like this. It feels like forever since I've touched a holding hand *period*. I didn't realize how starved I've been for affection until now.

I wonder how his hands would feel on my body ...

I pull away before I start humping his leg like a dog. "So, are you really a CEO?"

"Something like that. I actually got a promotion today. Hence the suit."

"Congratulations. What do you—"

"Are we gonna dance or what?" Kerry interrupts.

I smile up at Jaxon. "My friends are heathens, as you can see."

He laughs. "Dance with your friends. I'm not going anywhere."

I arch an eyebrow. *Why?* I want to ask. Why waste your time on me when you can have any girl in this place eating out of the palm of your hand?

Kerry yanks me away from him before I can say anything, and I'm pulled into the middle of the dance floor.

"That man is *fine*," Andrea shouts over the music.

Sammi nods eagerly. "He looks really into you."

Becca nudges me with her elbow. "Did you get his number?"

"The only thing I got was whiplash. Why did you pull me over here like that? We were in the middle of a conversation."

Kerry rolls her eyes. "You need to play hard to get. Make him work for it."

"Work for what?"

"You know what."

I shake my head. "I can't go home with him."

"Why not?" Mary asks. "No harm in it if you're careful."

"You wasted your twenties with ass face," Andrea says. "You're getting a second chance now. Have fun. Let loose."

"Have sex." Kerry wiggles her eyebrows.

Sex with a stranger? Can I do that? I've only had sex while in monogamous relationships. Would I be able to bare my body to someone I don't know for one night?

I look to Sammi for backup, but she shrugs. "If you're going to have sex with a random, do it with that guy."

I scoff. "So much for being the goody-two-shoes of our group."

"What? He's gorgeous."

I laugh. *That he is.* "Let's just dance and enjoy your kid-free night out."

"Say it louder for the mamas in the back!" Andrea raises her arms overhead and gyrates her hips.

We giggle and dance the night away in our impenetrable circle. I lose track of how many shots we down. It feels *so* good to enjoy myself without having to check the time. Andrew would get angry whenever I went out with the girls. Once nine o'clock hit, he'd send text after text, demanding I come home.

So I did.

Disgust racks through my body. *God*, when did I become this passive, meek woman? No wonder I gained weight. I stopped taking care of myself, too busy catering to Andrew's wants and needs.

What about *my* needs?

Why did I allow them to take a back seat?

Why did I let someone else dictate how my life should go?

An explosion goes off within me.

It's an awakening.

Or maybe it's just the alcohol.

Whatever it is, I know one thing for certain: Never again will I be the person I was in that marriage.

From this moment on, I'm going to do the things *I* want to do. Say the things *I* want to say. And I'm going to take the things *I* want to have.

No apologies.

No backing down.

I'm going to live the life *I* want.

I glance at Jaxon, who's watching me from his stool at the bar.

It's going to start tonight.

Everything's about to change.

CHAPTER FOUR

Jaxon

"She's seriously hot. Did you call dibs yet? Because if not, dibs."

I shoot Dan a glare that reads *hands off, motherfucker.*

His hands raise on either side of his blond head. "Roger that."

Shaun jerks his thumb toward the balloons. "Divorced chicks are awesome in bed. They've got all that pent-up frustration from being unhappy with their husbands for so long."

Smith shakes his head. "It's disturbing that you know this."

"What can I say? I have a type."

Dan chuckles. "Is that how you found Carrie on Match? Short male with small dick looking for sexually frustrated divorcee."

"Fuck you." Shaun tips his beer back and then sets the empty bottle onto the bar. "I'm going to take a piss."

I turn to Dan. "You know he's touchy about his height."

Dan waves me off. "Pfft. He's fine. His ego is big enough to withstand it."

My eyes drift over to Raegan. Again. They've been drawn to her since the second she walked into the bar. Gorgeous face. Long blond hair. Tight jeans. Full tits spilling out of her top. She has everything it takes to catch a man's attention. But that's not hard to do. Wave any scrap of food in front of a dog, he'll start to salivate.

The real feat is *keeping* a man's attention. And Raegan's keeping mine for three reasons.

Reason One: She read me and my friends like a book. She's perceptive, which tells me she's smart. Intelligence is sexy to a man.

Notice how I said *to a man*. If a guy's intimidated by a woman's brain, it means he's insecure about his own intelligence. Also, he probably has a small pecker.

Reason Two: Raegan was embarrassed by the balloons her friends brought her. She doesn't want her personal business to be put on display, which shows she isn't an attention-seeker. I'm not into narcissists. Been there, done that.

Reason Three: She's confident. This is where people tend to get confused. Some women claim to be confident when in reality, they're just plain rude. There's a difference between confident and conceited.

Raegan looked me in the eye and smiled, but didn't act like she was better than anyone. She wasn't trying to be sexy or funny. Plus, there was something honest in her eyes. Vulnerable. Maybe the hurt in me sensed the hurt within her.

Needless to say, I'm intrigued.

"Are you going to dance with her, or are you going to stare at her like some creeper?" Dan asks.

"I'm giving her space. She's with her friends."

"Don't wait too long. You don't want someone else taking her home at the end of the night."

I arch an eyebrow. "She might not want to be taken home by anyone at the end of the night."

"She will if you play your cards right."

"I don't need to play games to get a girl."

"Well, you need to do something," he says. "I know your hand is tired of jerking off in the shower every night."

"First of all," Shaun says, back from the bathroom, "how do you know he jerks off in the shower every night?"

"Jealous?"

Shaun laughs. "Hardly. But he has a point, Jax. It's been long enough. Don't you think it's time you broke your dry spell?"

I drain the rest of my beer. "I think you guys worry too much about my dick."

"Or you're not worried enough." Shaun claps me on the back. "I hate that bitch for doing such a number on you, man."

My stomach clenches at the reminder. "Change the subject."

"All right, all right. I'm just saying—"

"You've said plenty. Your turn to get the next round." Smith nudges Shaun toward the bar.

I give Smith an appreciative nod.

"You know he's just worried about you," Smith says. "We all are."

"Look, I wanted to come out tonight to celebrate, not to talk about my past. My life is finally back on track. I don't need to be reminded of my failures."

"You didn't fail at anything," Dan says. "None of what happened was your fault."

"I'm not having this conversation. It's over. I've moved on."

"Have you?"

"I have." My jaw ticks. "Now drop it."

"Consider it dropped."

I know the guys are looking out for me. I'd do the same for them. My ex-girlfriend shattered my heart and ran away with the pieces. I'd tried to fuck the memories away, did the whole different-girl-every-night thing. Nothing worked. If anything, random slutty women only reminded me of the she-devil more.

So I swore off women altogether. I threw myself into work, got my administrator's degree, and today I landed my dream job.

I'm finally on the upswing.

My eyes lock with Raegan across the room and the smile spreads across my face. It's been a while since I've felt drawn to a woman like this. A connection. She's a sign of all the good that's about to come my way. Maybe it's time to break my dry spell.

Dan takes the beer bottle out of my grip. "Stop creeping and go dance with her."

I shrug off my jacket and roll up my sleeves until they're halfway up my forearms. Raegan watches me as I make my way through the crowd. Anticipation dances in her eyes and I can tell she wants me as much as I want her.

Tonight, I'm letting go of the past. I'm dropping the pain and heartache like an anchor, and I'm abandoning ship.

Everything's about to change.

I slide behind Raegan and wrap my arms around her waist. She pushes her ass against me and moves her hips to the beat.

"Your friends are watching us," I whisper in her ear.

"So are yours."

"Guess we'd better give them a good show then."

Her cheeks flush, but her arms lift, weaving her fingers through my hair. She lays her head back onto my chest exposing her neck. I graze my lips against her silky skin and her grip on my hair tightens. She smells like a Caribbean vacation, coconut and pineapple.

We're swaying much slower than the music, oblivious in our own private bubble. Raegan tilts her head up and spears me with those green eyes—not a bright, emerald green, but a deeper, muted green. Like a forest. A forest where I could lie in the grass and lose myself for hours.

Her lips part and she pulls me down to them. When we kiss, it's as if the power in the room goes out. Everything's dark and all I can focus on is the way Raegan's luscious lips feel on mine, the warmth of her tongue dipping into my mouth.

Ever wonder what a man thinks about while kissing a woman? The way his dick will feel inside her mouth. Judging by the way Raegan's kissing me, I might be in for a treat. But I won't make the first move. If Raegan wants to come home with me, she'll have to let me know.

She pulls away, panting. "Let's get out of here."

And there it is.

I wait while she tells her friends. Then, taking her hand in mine, I barrel through the crowd like a freight train that's gone off the rails. Or at least, I'm moving as fast as I can with the throbbing hard-on in my pants.

When we reach my car outside, I push Raegan against the passenger door and claim her mouth again. She yanks my shirt, pulling the neatly tucked fabric out of my pants, and starts unbuttoning it. We're a frenzy of lips and hands searching for skin, like we'll die if we don't touch each other.

"Get in," I say.

On the ride to my apartment, it's a miracle I don't crash my car into a tree. Raegan kisses me the entire time, licking my neck, biting my earlobe. With one hand on the wheel, I slip the other into her jeans. She holds my wrist in place and rolls her hips, gliding my fingers over her wetness.

This woman is fucking my hand and it is the hottest thing I've ever seen.

I'm relieved when we reach my complex, because I'm seconds away from having to explain an embarrassing mess in my pants. I lift her out of the car and carry her inside my apartment, our lips fused together until I drop her onto my bed.

We scramble out of our clothes. I can't help but stare as she strips off her jeans and tosses her shirt onto the floor.

"God, you're sexy as hell." I reach behind her and unclasp her bra, freeing her tits so I can bury my face in them. She moans when I pull her nipple into my mouth and swirl my tongue around it. I do the same to the other one before trailing kisses down her stomach.

"I used to be more in-shape," she slurs, almost like an apology.

"You're perfect just like this." I'm not lying. Men don't want to fuck a stick. They want something to grip on to. Something to squeeze. Something that bounces and jiggles. You might be embarrassed of your muffin top, but the truth is: A man doesn't notice what's between your tits and your pussy when you're naked and his dick is about to be inside you.

I tug her panties to the side and skate my tongue over her bare skin. Raegan hooks her legs over my shoulders, blond hair splayed out on my navy comforter. Her hips buck up to meet every stroke of my tongue.

Did I say Raegan riding my hand was the hottest thing I'd ever seen? I was wrong. Raegan riding *my face* is the hottest thing I've ever seen.

Uninhibited. Unrestrained. She's enjoying every second of this, like she owns me and it's her right to take everything from me.

This is how sex *should* be.

It's not a sprint, a race to the finish line. It's about indulging your senses. A tasting. Exploring to find what you like, taking the time to enjoy every kiss, every touch, every movement.

This is what was missing from the random hookups I'd grown tired of.

Passion.

"Jaxon," she whimpers.

I love the sound of my name on her lips, the desperation in her voice. I drag the entire length of my tongue along her seam, circling around her clit. "What do you want, Raegan? Tell me what you need."

"I need ... I need ..."

Yes, I love it when women talk dirty.

"I need the bathroom."

My head jerks up. "What?"

She rolls off the bed and stumbles into the hallway, tripping over one of her shoes.

"First door on your right," I call after her.

The bathroom door slams shut, followed by the sounds of Raegan heaving into the toilet.

Awesome. My head drops onto the mattress.

So much for breaking my dry spell.

CHAPTER FIVE

Days Left Until School Starts: 29
Raegan

I am dying.

I yank the sheet over my eyes, hissing like a vampire who's being burned by the sun. I massage small circles on my temples. It feels as if someone's drilling a hole in my head. I try to swallow but my throat's too dry and scratchy. My hair is shellacked with sweat, sticking to my face and neck.

This has to be what death feels like.

I stretch my legs under the covers but my foot grazes something furry. I freeze.

I don't have any pets. What could be furry in my bed?

Tarantulas are furry. If there's a tarantula in here, I'm lighting the bed on fire.

Turning my head slowly to the side, I peel my eyelids open.

Oh ... my ... god.

The memories from last night flood my brain.

I'm not dying. I'm hungover. There isn't an arachnid in the bed. It's a man's leg.

Well, not just his leg. The rest of his body is attached to it. There aren't severed parts in my bed or anything.

Wait. This isn't *my* bed.

I peek out from under the covers. Navy comforter. Plain white walls. Mahogany dresser next to the closet. Clothes strewn about the dark laminate floor—specifically, my red lace thong and matching bra.

I lift the sheet up and assess my situation. Yup. I'm naked.

I had sex with Mr. Sexy in a Suit last night. This is his apartment. That leg belongs to him. He could wake up at any moment.

I think I'd prefer the tarantula.

I slither out of the bed and begin snatching pieces of my outfit off the floor. I pull my shirt over my head, slip my panties on, stuff my legs into my jeans, and toss my bra into my purse. Here's one shoe. *Where the hell is the other one?*

Fuck it. I can't stay here for one second longer. I'm out of the apartment so fast, there's probably a cartoon cloud of dust behind me.

I sprint down the stairs but my bare feet screech to a halt in the parking lot. *I don't have my car.* Groaning, I look to the sky as if someone up there is responsible for putting me in this situation.

I dig my phone out of my purse and scroll for Becca's name.

The piercing screams of her children sound before she answers, out of breath. "Hello?"

"Please tell me you can come pick me up right now."

"Why are you awake? It's six-thirty. Where's Jaxon? Why can't he drive you home?"

"Dude, I'm standing outside in my clothes from last night, I can't find my shoe, my hair looks like I stuck my head in a blender, and I'm pretty sure the man in this car rolling by thinks I'm a prostitute. I don't have time to answer your questions. This is an SOS!"

I can hear the amusement in her voice. "Jared's at the gym. I'll have to take the kids with me. Might take me a while to get out of the house."

"Hurry, Beck!"

"I have two toddlers. The word *hurry* left my vocabulary a long time ago."

"Okay, okay. Just get here. You're a life saver."

"What's the address?"

Squinting in the sunlight, my eyes dart around the apartment complex. "There's a big, white number four on the building I just came out of. It's a three-story brick building. Parking lot out front."

"You've just described every apartment complex in New Jersey. Look for a sign with the name of the place and text it to me."

When the call ends, I search the area. I step over a pile of broken glass and pray there's no rusty nails lying around. At least Cinderella had a horse and carriage to take her home when she lost *her* shoe. Lucky bitch.

After roaming around for several minutes, I spot a maroon sign with white lettering that reads *Ken Gardens Apartments*. I tap out a text to Becca and plop down onto the curb.

An elderly woman lugging her garbage bag to the dumpster shakes her head as she passes me.

"I'm not a prostitute!"

She scurries away with a horrified expression on her wrinkly face.

I bury my face in my hands and go through the clips I remember from last night's rendezvous. I drank way too much. That's obvious. I danced with Jaxon. Then he kissed me.

Good Lord, can that man kiss. My skin prickles at the crystal-clear memory of his mouth on mine.

But that's where everything gets hazy.

I can't remember anything that happened after that kiss.

"W<small>HAT DO YOU MEAN YOU CAN'T REMEMBER</small>?"

I rub my eyes with the heels of my hands. "It's like I have whore amnesia!"

Becca's daughter, Mia, giggles in the backseat as if she understands what I'm talking about.

"You're not a whore," Becca says. "Stop slut shaming yourself just because you had sex with a guy you met."

"Why did you let me go home with him?"

"Oh, no. No way. You are not pinning this one on me. I asked you what you wanted to do. I said, '*Are you sure you want to go home with him?*' and you said, '*I want to ride him like a bronco.*' Then I said—"

"Okay, I get it. It's not your fault." I let my head fall against the window. "I have sex with the hottest man I'll ever get and I can't even remember it. Figures."

"Sex!" Mia shouts. Her brother, William, pipes in and then the both of them chant, "Sex! Sex! Sex!"

"Great," Becca says. "You've turned my kids into whores too."

"Isn't that why you made me godmother?"

She giggles. "You're going to be fine, Rae. I know this was out of character for you, but you're allowed to unravel a little after everything you've been through. You were wound so tight with Andrew. Figure out who you are now. Do what makes you happy and forget about everything else."

"How did I get here?" I ask, more to myself than to Becca.

Becca takes a deep breath and blows it out through her lips before answering. "You did what we all do in a marriage. We want to please our husbands. We want to give them everything because we love them and we want them to be happy with us. But our husbands are supposed to give back. It's supposed to be an equal exchange of give and take." She shakes her head. "Some husbands don't know how to do that."

"You sound like you're talking from experience. Is everything okay between you and Jared?"

She hikes a shoulder. "You getting divorced has been an eye-opener for me."

"How so?"

"You stood up for yourself. You were unhappy and you changed your situation. I don't think I could be that strong. I don't know if I could open my mouth and say all the things I feel inside." She glances at me before turning her attention back to the road. "I admire you for that."

"Telling Andrew how unhappy I was ... that was the hardest thing I've ever had to do. I still don't know how the words came out." I place my hand on her arm and squeeze. "You have that strength inside you. You don't think you have it, but it's in there."

She swipes a fallen tear and smiles at her kids in the rear-view mirror. "He gave me two beautiful babies and that's all I can ask for."

We're silent for the remainder of the ride until Becca's car comes to a stop in front of my mom's house.

I swing my legs out of the car. "By the way, I'm telling Mom I slept at your house last night."

"You're thirty-years old. You don't have to tell her anything."

"It kinda feels like I do. I'm staying in her house. It's all a little weird right now."

"You'll be back on your feet in no time. Let me know when you're ready to go apartment hunting."

"And you let me know if you ever want to talk."

She nods. "Will do."

"Thanks for coming to get me." I gesture to my wrinkled ensemble. "I look like a walking one-night stand."

"That's why they call it the walk of shame." Becca winks and pulls away.

Staring up at the house I spent my childhood in, I square my shoulders. "Today is a new day. It's the first day of the rest of my life."

My mom swings open the door before my feet hit the porch. "I was worried when you didn't come home last night. Was that Becca who dropped you off?"

"Yes, it was. Sorry I didn't call. I drank a little too much and it was late. Didn't want to wake you."

Mom wraps her arms around me. "It's all right. I was hoping you met a nice guy and went home with him."

My face contorts into a disgusted expression. "What mother hopes her daughter had sex with a random stranger?"

"A mother who cares about her daughter. That's who." She ushers me into the kitchen and pulls out a chair at the table. The table is filled with pancakes, scrambled eggs, turkey bacon, and a bowl of fresh berries.

"Wow, Mom. This looks amazing."

"I know you said you wanted to get back in shape, so think of this as your last supper. I cleaned out the house last night. Fridge too. There isn't an ounce of junk food left."

My eyebrows lift. "You didn't have to do that for me."

She waves a hand and takes the seat next to me. "I've let myself go since your father passed. Now that you're living here, you and I can do this together and help each other."

"I guess we both like to eat when we feel stressed, huh?"

"You got that from me, unfortunately." She cups my face and smiles. "But you're young and beautiful, and I want you to be healthy."

Dad died three years ago from a massive heart attack that no one saw coming. I always hated thinking about Mom in this big house all by herself. As strange as it is to be back home, there's a part of me that's glad to be here. Both our hearts need mending, and no one can mend your heart quite like your mother can.

"So what's on the agenda today?" she asks as we dig into breakfast.

"I feel like death. I wanted to start working out today, but my new smokin' hot bod might have to wait until tomorrow."

"You should replenish your fluids and rest. Maybe later we can go food shopping and stock up on fruits and veggies."

"Sure. Why don't we go to the movies tonight? I know you've been dying to see that new JLo movie."

Mom's eyes light up and warmth spreads in my chest. I know I haven't spent as much time with her as I should. Now that the divorce is behind me, I can focus on the things that really matter.

Just because my marriage is over, doesn't mean my life has to be.

Mom raises her glass of orange juice. "To new beginnings."

I clink mine against hers and smile.

And to sexy men in suits who I'll never see again.

CHAPTER SIX

Jaxon

*M*y hand searches the spot beside me for Raegan. When I feel nothing but a cold sheet, my eyes pop open. *Where is she?*

"Raegan?"

Silence.

I flip the covers off my body and swing my legs out of bed. My clothes are in a heap on the floor where I left them, but hers are not entangled with mine.

I shuffle down the hall. "Raegan, you sick again?"

The bathroom door is open, light off. I check the living room and kitchen, but Raegan is nowhere to be found.

As I head back to my bedroom, my gaze lands on a black high heel twisted in the corner of my comforter on the floor.

Huh. That's a first. Normally, I can't get the girl out the next morning. But this one? No goodbye. No awkward *can I get your number and call you sometime?* She left in such a hurry, she didn't even bother to put on her other shoe. Is she trying to act out some weird Cinderella fantasy?

I reach for my phone on the nightstand. Let's see if she stored her number before she left.

No such luck.

I crawl back into bed and lay flat on my back, staring up at the ceiling. An odd sense of disappointment settles into my chest. Odd because I don't know anything about the girl. Odd because we didn't even have sex. Raegan is nothing more than a random woman I brought home from a bar. I shouldn't care that she's gone.

But there was just something about her. Something that made her seem like more than a random woman I brought home from a bar.

Either way, she's gone, so I head to the shower and go about my day.

Later while I'm changing my sheets, my dad's picture pops up on my phone. I click the green button and hold the phone between my ear and my shoulder. "Hi, Dad."

"Jaxon. Just calling to make sure you're coming to dinner tonight."

"I'll be there. Does Mom want me to bring anything?"

"Just your handsome self!" she calls from somewhere in the background.

What is it with parents always talking to you on speaker phone?

"Bring Nana's ring," Dad says. "I talked to Harry at work. He said his brother-in-law is a jeweler and can take a look at it."

"I already told you, I'm not hocking it."

"I know, I know. But we should have it appraised."

"Why does it matter how much it is?"

"If it's worth a lot of money, we can have it insured in case it's ever lost or damaged."

"I'll never lose it." My eyes flick to the blue velvet ring box on my dresser where I put it the other day.

Only it's not there.

My heart sinks down into my stomach. Dad's rambling on but all I can hear is the blood pounding in my ears.

Where the fuck is my grandmother's ring?

"All right, Dad. Gotta run. I'll see you at six." I end the call and toss my phone onto the mattress. Dropping to my knees, I look under the bed. Nothing but dust bunnies.

Next, I pull the dresser away from the wall. Maybe the ring box fell behind it.

Nope.

I search the drawers and scour the room, only to come up empty-handed.

I thrust my fingers through my hair, pacing at the foot of my bed. "Okay. I just need to retrace my steps. Everything's fine."

FYI: Talking to yourself solidifies that everything is *not* fine.

Nana passed away last month. It took me and my family weeks to sort through her belongings at her house. There wasn't much of value there besides a couple boxes of pictures. But when the family lawyer read Nana's will, we learned she'd left her wedding ring to me.

My brother, Josh, was livid. Nearly started a family feud over the thing. He wanted to give the ring to his current flavor of the week. Apparently, they're *in love*. I'm not one to shit on people's relationships, but Josh is the boy who cried love.

Dad didn't buy it any more than I did, and he told Josh that I get the ring since I'm the oldest. We all know the real reason Nana left it to me. Josh would pawn the ring, blow the money, and never think twice about it. He's the typical irresponsible little brother.

I'm the responsible one.

I'm the dependable one.

Don't think I don't see the irony in this situation as I'm crawling around my apartment on my hands and knees.

After the lawyer gave me the ring, I set the box on top of my dresser. Smack in the middle. I've been meaning to buy a safe or a lockbox to put it in, but things have been hectic ever since I interviewed for the new job.

I'd forgotten about the ring. But I hadn't touched it, so it has to be here.

I spend the rest of my afternoon tearing the place apart. I check in the most ridiculous places, knowing damn well it wouldn't be inside the oven or behind the toilet.

I'd put it in my room. On my dresser. Yet it's not here.

My minds drifts to thoughts of Raegan. Only this time, instead of images of her smile, her eyes, or her naked body, it ends up on a grim discovery.

Did Raegan steal the ring?

I've taken plenty of girls back to my apartment over the years. Never have I been robbed. But my grandmother's ring is gone, and coincidentally, so is Raegan. Maybe she left because she took something that didn't belong to her. She saw an opportunity and seized it while I was asleep.

Call me naïve, but I didn't get that vibe from Raegan. I know she was a stranger, but she seemed like a sweet girl. Genuine.

Turns out she's nothing but a con artist. She didn't even have to sleep with me to get what she wanted.

Guess I'm a sucker for a pretty face.

The thought settles into my mind like a planted seed.

Raegan stole the ring.

How am I going to explain this one to Dad?

MY HAND SHAKES AS I TURN THE KNOB TO ENTER MY PARENTS' house.

The delicious scent of garlic fills my nostrils, but my stomach doesn't growl like it normally does. I'm about to tell my father that his mother's ring, our family heirloom, has been stolen.

All because I couldn't keep my dick in my pants.

"You're late, Golden Boy." Josh strides toward the entryway, beer already in hand.

I level my brother with a look. "I told you not to call me that."

"Which is exactly why I do."

I roll my eyes and shoulder past him to find Dad.

At the end of the hallway, the door to Dad's office is open. I knock on the doorframe and step inside.

He glances in my direction before returning his eyes to his computer screen. "Is dinner ready? I'm almost done."

I close the door and lock it so Josh won't be able to barge in. He's the last person I want to hear the news I'm about to break to Dad.

"I need to talk to you about something." I take a seat in the leather chair opposing Dad's large oak desk.

He swivels in his chair to face me and folds his hands on the desk. "What's wrong?"

Releasing a shaky breath, I blurt it out before I lose my nerve. "I can't find Nana's ring."

His eyebrows pinch together. "What do you mean you can't find it?"

I run my fingers through my hair, pulling at the ends in frustration. "I've looked everywhere for it. I thought I left it on my dresser, but this morning I woke up and it's gone."

His mouth hangs open for what feels like an eternity. "That's impossible. If it was on your dresser, it couldn't've gone anywhere. Did you search the room?"

"I turned the entire apartment upside-down. It's not there."

"How can that be?"

I swallow past the boulder lodged in my throat. "I brought a girl home last night. When I woke up, she was gone."

"What does this have to do with ..." His words trail off as his brain connects the missing pieces.

I cover my face with both hands and a strangled groan escapes from my throat. "I'm not sure she took it, but it would explain how the ring went missing."

"Of course she took it." Dad's face reddens, and I can hear the disappointment in his voice. "You need to call the police."

"And say what? A girl might've stolen my grandmother's ring, but I don't know who she is or where she lives?"

Dad sets his glasses on the desk and scrubs a hand over his face. "Can't you call her?"

I look down at my lap when I say, "We didn't exchange numbers."

Dad sighs and rocks back in his chair. "This is something I'd expect from Josh."

I cringe. "I know."

"We can't tell your mother about this."

I nod. "What should I do?"

"File a report with the police. Notify any pawn shops in the area. If that girl stole your ring, she's looking for money. As for your mother and Josh," he says, pushing out of his chair. "You tell them nothing."

I hate lying. Despise it. I'd been on the receiving end of a huge, dirty lie once, and I've vowed never to make anyone feel like that. Now I have to lie to the most important people in my life.

Anger, pain, regret, and guilt swell, creating the perfect storm inside my gut.

I make a new promise to myself: If I ever lay eyes on Raegan again, I'm going to make her pay.

CHAPTER SEVEN

Days Left Until School Starts: 2

Raegan

"*I* can't believe we're back. It feels like summer just started."

Andrea groans. "It always goes by too quickly. Two months is not enough of a break for all the hard work we put in during the other ten months."

"I wonder who our new principal is going to be." I click my pen as I look around the faculty room. "Everyone in here is chomping at the bit."

"Hey, Rae." Chris, the school's physical education teacher, waves from the next table. "How was your summer?"

"It was good. How was yours?"

"Not bad. Went by too fast, of course. You look great."

I smile as my cheeks redden. "Thanks. Lost some weight."

Several teachers turn around to survey me. I sit up a little straighter in my chair. Between meal prepping, running, and kickboxing, I'd worked my ass off this summer. Lost fifteen pounds.

Take that, Andrew.

Not that I did it for him. I did it for me. I don't want to die early from unhealthy eating.

Take that, diabetes.

Susan Faye, one of the veteran teachers at our school, offers me a sad smile. "I heard about your divorce. Welcome to the club."

I cringe inwardly. "Thanks, Sue."

"You gonna ditch us for the divorcee's club?" Kerry whispers.

I roll my eyes. Before I can answer, the door swings open and our new principal strides into the room.

Mary and Andrea fist-bump under the table. "Finally, a male principal," Andrea whispers.

Tall, lean frame. Perfectly-fitting dark grey suit with a pastel pink shirt underneath. *I love when men wear pink.* My eyes drag up his body until they reach his flawless, tan—*wait*, I recognize that face.

And all the air leaves my lungs.

Holyshitmotherfuckingcocksuckerasscrack.

I must be dreaming.

This has to be a dream.

There is no way my one-and-only-one-in-my-whole-life-night stand is my new boss.

They say to pinch yourself if you're dreaming, right?

Ouch. Nope. Jaxon is still standing at that podium.

"Is she breathing?" Kerry whispers.

"I don't know," Andrea says. "Beck, hold a mirror under her nose."

Becca leans in. "You okay, Rae?"

My eyes remain locked on him. "What is *he* doing here?"

"Looks like he's our new principal."

I tear my eyes away and cover my face with my hands. This *cannot* be happening. "I'll have to dye my hair. Maybe just shave it all off. I can wear a disguise all year, right?"

"My cousin can make you a sick hunchback." Kerry nods, completely serious. "It'll look real, I swear."

"You'd look hot as a redhead," Mary chimes in.

I use the back of my pen to scratch my thigh. I always break out in hives whenever I get anxious. Maybe I won't need the disguise after all. I'll be so red and blotchy, Jaxon won't be able to recognize me.

I steal another glance in his direction. He's spotted me, and the way he's staring at me confirms that he does recognize me.

Shit, shit, shit, shit, shit, shit, shit.

"Maybe he won't remember you," Kerry whispers.

Mary shakes her head. "He definitely remembers her. Look at that smirk."

Becca points to my lap. "Rae, your leg!"

The pen I was scratching myself with—the one I thought I'd clicked closed—was open. As if this moment couldn't get any more humiliating for me, there are now black zigzags drawn all over my knee.

Mary snatches the pen from my grip while Sammi digs a tissue out of her purse and dips it into her water bottle.

I scrub my leg, but the ink only smears. "What is this, permanent ink?"

"Try this." Becca squirts hand sanitizer on my thigh.

I rub the clear gel into my skin and an intense heat creeps up my leg. "This fucking burns, Becca."

"I'm sorry!"

Andrea dabs lotion onto my leg. "This might help the burning."

I swat her hand away. "Okay, can we stop mixing random shit on my body, please?"

Our heads jerk up when we hear the sound of chairs scraping against the floor. Everyone is standing and heading towards the door. The meeting must be over.

I shoot up out of my seat. "I have to get out of here before he—"

"Raegan?"

His deep voice sends a shiver down my spine. There's no escape. It's time to face the music.

I spin on my heels and force a smile. "Jaxon. I mean, Mr. Waters. Or is it Dr. Waters? Are you a doctor? You look too young to have your doctorate. Then again, I look too young to be divorced and here I am. But you knew that already. Unless you don't remember. I don't remember much from that night, to be honest. That'll be the last time I drink like that. I haven't had a drink since actually. Wow. I guess this was the job you were celebrating." I laugh, trying to seem nonchalant but a strange, high-pitched sound escapes my throat—something like a cross between a bird and a hyena.

"Someone find her off switch," Kerry whispers.

Jaxon grins. His hair is perfectly quaffed, lips smooth as butter. He oozes power and control. The man is gorgeous.

And here I am with blotches all over my skin and ink scribbled onto my leg like a damn toddler.

"It's Mr. Waters. No doctorate yet. But you can call me Jax." He turns to the girls. "Nice to see you again, ladies."

"Hi, Jax." Mary nudges Becca. "Let's leave these two to talk. We have a lot of work to do in our rooms."

My friends scurry out of the room despite my pleading eyes.

"Didn't think I'd ever see you again," Jaxon says.

"Trust me, neither did I."

"Almost thought I'd dreamed it." He chuckles and rubs the back of his neck. "I woke up and you were gone."

My cheeks flame. "I figured it would be easier if I left. Didn't want things to be awkward."

"Why would it be awkward?"

"I know this might sound cliché but I've never done anything like that before."

"Like that?" he echoes.

"Sex with a stranger. I thought it'd be weird in the morning. I was pretty mortified when I woke up."

His eyebrow arches. "You really don't remember what happened?"

"Sorry. I know that must not feel great for your ego."

"We didn't have sex, Raegan."

My mouth pops open. "But we went back to your apartment. I woke up completely naked in your bed."

He chuckles. "I was going down on you but you ran to the bathroom and threw up. You were in there for half the night before I carried you to bed."

My hand flies up to cover my mouth and my eyes squeeze shut. *Unbelievable.* The universe sends me the sexiest man alive, and I puke and pass out. "I am so sorry."

He shakes his head. "Don't worry about it."

I offer him a sheepish smile. "Thanks for not taking advantage of me in my drunken state."

"Of course. What kind of lowlife person would I be if I took advantage of a girl while she was drunk?" He edges closer and trails his fingers down my arm. "But I guess someone like you would expect that sort of thing."

My spine stiffens as my eyes flick up to his. "What?"

His fingers wrap around my wrist and tighten. "You know all about taking advantage of someone, don't you, Raegan?"

CHAPTER EIGHT

Jaxon

I'd practiced my first speech as principal for a month straight. I wrote it on index cards and recited the lines in the mirror. When I walked into the faculty room today, I felt prepared.

What I hadn't been prepared for was seeing Raegan sitting amongst the faculty.

It's not the long, blond hair that slaps me with recognition. Not the luscious lips, or the perfect pair of tits stretching against the straps of her tank top.

No. It's the wide green eyes blinking at me in shock.

The ones filled with fear and guilt.

They're the eyes of a thief who's been caught.

I tried to play it cool when I approached her, but I couldn't stop myself from reaching out and seizing her arm.

"You know all about taking advantage of someone, don't you, Raegan?"

"What are you talking about?" Raegan pulls her arm back, but I only tighten my grip.

I can't believe what a good actress she is. She must get away with this shit all the time. "Drop the act. We both know what you did. What you took."

"Please let go of me, Jaxon. I don't know what you think I took but I can assure you, I don't have anything that belongs to you."

I bark out a laugh. "You sound believable, you really do. You sure as shit had me fooled. How many other guys have you done this to? How much have you made from this little game?"

Her eyebrows pinch together and her jaw clenches. "I don't know what you're talking about, but if you don't let go of me, I'm going to scream."

What am I doing? This isn't me. I don't put my hands on women. Even if she is a cunning little thief. I drop her wrist and take a step back.

Raegan bolts to the door and disappears into the hallway before I can say another word. She could go straight to Human Resources and I'd lose my job in a heartbeat. I need to be smart about this. I have no proof that she stole anything from me. It's her word against mine.

But the universe practically put Raegan in my lap. I have a chance to get that ring back. Just need to figure out how to get her to confess that she stole it.

She thought she could get away with her little disappearing act. But this is *my* school. I'm her boss, and she's going to have to play by my rules.

CHAPTER NINE

Raegan

"*W*hat the hell am I going to do?"

The girls are just as shocked as I am, watching me pace the floor in Becca's classroom.

"Do you have any bruising?" Kerry asks.

I turn my wrist over and shake my head. "No. He didn't squeeze me that hard."

She shrugs. "We can help you with that."

"What are you suggesting?" Mary asks.

"I'm just saying, the guy's obviously a psychopath. If Rae shows up at the admin building with bruises on her arm, Jaxon will be fired so fast it'll make his head spin."

"It could also ruin his life." Sammi turns to me. "What does he think you stole?"

I spread my arms out wide. "I have no idea! This is insane. How am I supposed to work with a guy that's convinced I took something from him after our night of almost-sex together?"

Silence again.

Andrea stands. "Why don't we go confront him together? We'll be your witnesses. Maybe you two can have a civil conversation and clear up this obvious misunderstanding." She pushes her knuckles against her palms until they crack. "And if he tries anything, we'll kick his ass."

"Simmer down, Black Widow." Kerry nudges her with her elbow. "We need to be smart about this. He's our principal now. He can make our lives miserable for the next one-hundred and eighty days."

I groan, sinking into a kid-sized chair. "This school year is off to a horrible start and it hasn't even begun."

"This is the last thing you need to worry about." Becca runs her fingers through her hair, and I can see the wheels spinning in her mind. "In two days, over 120 five-year olds are going to storm through those doors and our awesome summer lives will be over. I say you go in your room, pretend like this never happened, and prepare for the school year. You told Jax you didn't steal anything. Maybe he'll drop it."

I chew my bottom lip. "I don't know. He seemed pretty angry."

"It's your word against his. He has no proof. He has no solid leg to stand on. If he lost something, that's on him."

"She's right, Rae." Kerry stands and pushes in her chair. "Let's go set up our rooms and forget about him. We've got work to do."

"Keep your doors open, ladies," Andrea says. "If Principal Fuckwad comes down this hallway, we'll hear him."

I walk next door to my classroom in a daze. There's so much to do to set up for the upcoming school year, but I can't concentrate on anything.

Here I thought all I'd have to worry about was explaining my maiden name to my co-workers. But my divorce pales in comparison to *this*.

My boss thinks I stole something from his apartment.

My boss who saw me naked.

My boss who went down on me.

Things just went from bad to worse.

PRINCIPAL FUCKWAD STAYED AWAY FROM ME FOR THE REMAINDER OF the day.

I set up half of my classroom, but the rest will have to wait until tomorrow. I'm exhausted and just want to go home.

The girls and I are about to leave when we pass the main office, and my conscience tugs me back. "I think I'm going to try to talk to Jaxon one more time."

"I don't think that's a good idea," Sammi says.

"I'm not going to be able to sleep tonight with this weighing on my mind. Maybe he's had some time to calm down."

"Or maybe he's waiting for you to leave so he can shove you into the trunk of his car."

Our heads whip around to look at Kerry.

"What?" she asks. "It happens."

"Girl, you need to stop watching all those Netflix documentaries," Mary says, shaking her head.

"We'll wait here for you." Andrea places her hand on my shoulder. "If anything happens, we'll be right outside this door."

I salute them before walking into the main office. Jaxon's door is closed, so I rap three times on the wood.

"Come in," his deep voice calls.

I peek my head inside Jaxon's office. He's sitting behind stacks of papers piled high on his desk. His hair is mussed, like he ran his fingers through it countless times. His tie is loosened, top button of his shirt undone. He seems stressed. Being the principal is a job I'd never want. The politics, the responsibility, the endless workload. I'll take the classroom over the office any day.

As soon as Jaxon sees me, his expression hardens.

I fiddle with the hem of my dress. "Do you have a minute?"

He leans back in his chair and folds his hands in his lap. "Come to confess?"

Heat pools in my chest. *Stay calm, Rae.* More bees with honey and all. "I was hoping you'd cooled down so we could chat like civilized human beings." I rub my wrist as a warning. A small threat of blackmail never hurt anybody.

His cocky façade fades. He gestures to the chair in front of his desk. "Have a seat."

Point for me. I lower myself into the chair and cross my legs. "I have to ask: What happened to give you the impression that I stole something from you?"

Anger flashes in his eyes but his voice is even when he speaks. "The night you came to my apartment, I had my grandmother's ring in a box on my dresser." He shifts in his seat. "She passed recently."

"I'm sorry for your loss." I search my memory for any recollection of seeing something on his dresser. I'd left in such a hurry that morning, I didn't stop to take inventory of his bedroom. I didn't even stay long enough to retrieve my shoe. "I remember what your dresser looks like, but I can't remember seeing anything on it before I left that day."

He smirks. "How convenient. You don't remember."

Breathe. Don't let his attitude fluster you. "Was the ring there when I got to your apartment that night?"

"Of course it was there. I put it there."

"But you're sure it was there when we came back from the bar?"

"Where else would it be? It's not like it could've gotten up and moved. Not until you swiped it and ran out."

My hands ball into fists. "I did not take your grandmother's ring. You know, I couldn't find my shoe that morning either. Maybe your ring is somewhere with my shoe. Did you check under the bed, or behind the dresser?"

He pinches the bridge of his nose. "Yes, Nancy Drew. I checked every square inch of that apartment and the ring is nowhere to be found."

His snarky comment reminds me of Andrew. Acid trickles into my stomach. I might've felt bad for the fact that this guy lost his late grandmother's ring, but I'm done playing nice. This stops here.

"So, you don't know if the ring was actually there at the same time I was. You have no proof of what you're accusing me of. And you put your hands on a staff member." I stand and cross my arms over my chest. "Sounds like a closed case to me, Mr. Waters."

His nostrils flare as he pushes out of his seat. "That ring has been passed down in my family for generations. It means something to us. So I hope you can sleep at night knowing you stole something so precious from me."

"Like I said, I didn't steal your grandmother's ring. I'm sorry you lost it, but I don't have it. So I'll sleep very well, thanks."

His top lip curls as he looks me up and down. "I'm glad I didn't end up sleeping with you. You getting sloppy drunk actually did me a favor."

"The feeling is mutual." I spin on my heels but whip back around when I reach the door. "And I'd like my shoe back tomorrow."

"You'll get your shoe when I get my—"

I slam the door on my way out and whiz past the girls waiting for me in the hallway. Their flip-flops smack the floor behind me as they try to keep up with my pace.

"What happened?"

"Did he touch you?"

"Does he believe you didn't steal anything?"

"Why does he have your shoe?"

I push through the double doors at the main entrance and inhale the sweet scent of lingering summer air. Closing my eyes, I collect my thoughts and try to slow my rapid heartbeat.

"He thinks I stole his grandmother's ring. He said it was in his bedroom the night he brought me home, and that it was gone when he woke up the next morning."

"That's ridiculous," Kerry says. "He obviously misplaced it and now he feels like an idiot so he's blaming you."

Becca chews on her bottom lip. "This is crazy. Maybe the guy's not right in the head."

"He's too good-looking," Andrea says. "Something was bound to be wrong with him."

I shrug. "I've said my peace. There's nothing I can do to prove that I didn't steal his ring."

"What are you going to do now?" Sammi asks.

"First, I'm going for a run. Then, I'm going to enjoy a nice dinner with my mother."

"And what about Principal Fuckwad?"

"He's just going to have to get over it."

This is my *school.*

CHAPTER TEN

Days Left Until Summer Break: 179
Jaxon

"Yes, Mrs. Zuckerman. I am positive it was your son who smeared feces on the bathroom walls."

There's a sentence I never thought I'd say.

"We have video surveillance of Andrew exiting the bathroom at the time of the offense. Yes, I'd appreciate it if you spoke to him about the importance of bathroom hygiene at home. Thank you. You have a wonderful day."

I place the receiver down and massage my scalp with my fingers.

"The first day is always the hardest," Beth, my secretary, calls from the main office.

"Somehow, that doesn't comfort me." I step out of my office and dangle a mini Snickers bar in front of Beth's face. "Want one?"

She snatches it out of my hands and devours it within seconds. Not completely sure she didn't inhale the wrapper with it.

The most important lesson too many principals fail to learn: The secretary and custodial staff are your best allies. Spoil them and they will do anything for you.

"I'm going to make my rounds," I say. "I've got the walkie if you need me."

"Have fun. Show those kids who's boss."

I shoot her a wink before striding into the hallway.

Second grade is in the cafeteria eating lunch. As a kid, lunchtime is your favorite time of day. As a teacher, it's the only time you get to go to the bathroom, check your texts, make copies, and scarf down your food. It's the *only* time you get to sit and catch your breath, and it's over in a flash.

And if you have lunch duty? Cut that precious time in half because the other half will be spent supervising over one-hundred students in the lunchroom. That job could scare even the badass Dwayne Johnson. I'd like to see him handle a kid with a bloody nose, with another student who's crying because he doesn't like the turkey sandwich his mother gave him, while two other students start a food fight.

I stick my head through the doorway and make eye-contact with the teacher on duty. "Everything okay?"

She nods and gives me a thumbs up. Then a little boy runs up to her, pinching his fly, doing what we refer to as The Pee-Pee Dance.

Why kids always wait until the last second to ask for the bathroom, I'll never understand.

I continue down the hall, waving to the physical education teacher and the librarian as I pass their rooms. Then I pop in to each first-grade classroom, wishing the students a great first day.

When I turn the corner, I'm in the kindergarten hallway. My stride slows as I approach the first room.

Raegan's room.

I haven't seen Raegan since she left my office two days ago. She won't admit to stealing my ring, and I won't believe that she didn't steal it. We're at a stalemate. At this point, there's nothing more I can do. Not until I can figure out a way to get her to confess.

And I *will* get her to confess.

I need that ring back. There's no other option.

Her door's open, so I lean against the frame. The class is sitting in a circle on the rug. In a rocking chair with a crying child sitting in her lap, Raegan's reading a story and trying to make her voice heard above the wailing student while consoling him at the same time.

Kindergarten teachers are the toughest kind of teachers there are. They take a class of five-year-olds, most who've never been in school before, and transform them into responsible, respectful, well-mannered students. And while they're teaching them how to share, and why they shouldn't pick their noses and eat it, they also teach them how to read and write.

Have you ever tried to teach someone the English language? It's the hardest thing you'll ever do.

As if the job isn't difficult enough, there are the occasional students who need to be evaluated for special education. The process is long, and the parents aren't always on board. This means the teachers have to manage some pretty extreme behaviors while attempting to meet the needs of every other student in her class.

It's like juggling chainsaws, and someone keeps throwing you more to juggle.

Raegan's eyes meet mine as I enter her classroom. She's in a yellow sundress, her golden hair cascading in loose curls down past her shoulders. She doesn't wear heavy make-up. She doesn't need to. The woman radiates natural beauty. My dick stirs as I recall what she looks like underneath that dress.

Down, boy. She's the enemy. Plus, I'm surrounded by children who wouldn't hesitate to point out my erection.

Raegan lays the book she's reading face-down in her lap and smiles wide. "Class, say Good Morning to Principal Waters."

The class shouts, "Good Morning Principal Waters."

"He is in charge of our whole school," Raegan says.

"Are you like the president?" a little girl asks.

I chuckle. "I'm the president of our school."

"Well then maybe you can help Joshua. He's been crying since we came to school this morning. I think he misses his mommy."

I kneel down beside her. "That's very kind of you to ask for help for your friend. What's your name?"

"Hannah."

"All right, Hannah. Let's see what we can do about your friend." I lower myself onto the carpet and crisscross my legs. Not an easy task in a suit, but kids learn from example. I hold my arms out toward the crying boy in Raegan's lap. "Joshua, come sit with me."

The room is silent while Joshua climbs down from the rocking chair and into my arms. I rub his back in slow circles. "What story are we reading, Hannah?"

"The Three Little Pigs," she says. "We're at the part where the wolf goes to the brick house."

"Oh, that's the best part." I nod at Raegan to continue, who's staring at me with a look of utter shock.

While she reads, I talk to Joshua in a low, soothing tone. "Your mommy called me before. She wanted me to check on you and give you a very important message."

Joshua's watery eyes look into mine. "She did?"

I nod. "She did. She told me to tell you that she is so proud of you for coming to this big boy school. She can't wait to hear about all the fun things you did on your first day. I told her I'd let her know how you're doing. But I don't want to tell her that you've been crying all morning. That would make mommy sad. What do you think I should tell her?"

Joshua sniffles as he ponders for a moment. "Maybe you can tell her I'm listening to a story."

"That's a good idea. I'd also like to tell her you made a friend. Maybe you can sit here with Hannah. She is very nice."

Hannah smiles and pats the rug beside her.

"And you'll tell my mom I was being a good boy?" Joshua asks.

"I'll call her as soon as I leave this room."

Joshua slides off my lap and onto the carpet next to Hannah. She rubs his back the same way I did, and when they hear the part of the story when the wolf falls into the pot of boiling water, Joshua laughs.

Raegan's expression is priceless, her lips forming a little O-shape. She clearly underestimated my abilities. That makes me glad.

It'll be that much sweeter when I take back what's mine.

CHAPTER ELEVEN

Raegan

"*H*ow can someone that rude be so good with kids?" Kerry asks. "Aren't children supposed to sense bad people?"

"I think that's dogs," Andrea says.

"You should've seen him." I peel the lid off my yogurt. "He got Joshua to stop crying in two seconds. It's like he's the child whisperer or something."

"Send him to my room," says Mary. "I've got a crier too. Poor kid won't even eat her lunch."

It's only twelve o'clock, and we're already exhausted. Our pretty first day of school dresses are soaked in sweat. Our feet are throbbing. And we still have three hours left to go.

I can't stop thinking about how helpful Jaxon was with Joshua. He was ... sweet. It was the same Jaxon I'd met at the bar last month. Nothing like the unhinged version I'd gotten a front row seat to a couple of days ago.

Why did he help me? Maybe this means he doesn't think I stole his grandmother's ring after all. Maybe he came to his senses.

A knock at Becca's classroom door tears our attention away from our lunches. My stomach twists when I see Jaxon standing in the doorway.

"Just checking up on you ladies. Everybody surviving?"

We all groan in unison.

Jaxon chuckles. "You're doing a great job. The day's half over. Raegan, may I speak with you for a minute?"

I suck in a breath and smooth out my dress as I follow Jaxon into the hallway.

"I need you to be our mascot later during the assembly."

I choke and sputter in disbelief. "Are you kidding me?"

He crosses his arms over his chest, a smug smile on his stupid handsome face. "I helped you with Joshua this morning. Now I need you to do something for me."

My eyes narrow. *That's why he was so nice before.* "Who's going to sit with my class while I'm in the costume?"

"Chris can watch them. He doesn't have a class that period."

"So then why don't you ask Chris to be the mascot?"

"Because I'm in charge, and I want *you* to be the mascot."

We stare each other down, a battle of the wills. In the end, I have no choice but to back down. He's my boss. If I want to keep my job, I have to do what he says.

"Fine." I spin around and stomp back into Becca's room.

"Everything all right?" Sammi asks.

"Sure. Everything's great. You're looking at the mascot for today's assembly."

"Are you okay in there?"

"I'm in a giant bird costume. It's a thousand degrees in here. And I can't see where I'm going. I am definitely not okay."

The Vice Principal, Mrs. Wilcox, laughs. "It was great of you to volunteer to do this. It's like pulling teeth trying to find someone willing to put this thing on."

"Can't imagine why," I mutter.

"Once Mr. Waters calls you in, you're going to walk straight down the middle of the auditorium. I will hold your wing and guide you, since you can't see. You'll dance a little at the front until the music stops, wave a few times. That's it. It'll be five minutes tops."

Beads of sweat trickle down my cheeks. Five minutes. I can do this.

The auditorium erupts in cheers. "That's your cue. Here we go."

I shuffle my giant bird feet, allowing Mrs. Wilcox to guide me down the aisle. She says something to me, but the music's so loud, I can't hear her. All I can do is keep moving. Just a few more minutes and this will be over.

As I take my next step, my foot hits something. I lose my balance and start to fall forward. I flap my wings around, trying to steady myself, but it's no use. I tip over and hit the ground.

The music stops and the crowd gasps. I roll over, trying to build enough momentum to pull myself up. But like a turtle stuck on its back, I can't get to my feet. *Where the hell is Mrs. Wilcox?*

"You stepped on my foot!" a kid yells.

Oh my God. I stepped on a student?

"Get the bird!" yells another.

"No!" I shriek. "Don't get the bird!"

Someone pounces on my stomach. Someone else kicks my leg. Before I can stop them, there's a gang of kids beating the crap out of me as I lie helpless on the ground.

"Ouch! Stop!" My arms and legs flail, kicking and pushing anyone who's near me. I don't care if they get hurt. It's every man for himself, and I will not be taken out by a pack of rabid children.

Finally, someone hoists me off the ground. I hear Jaxon's voice on the microphone, telling the students to take their seats.

The asshole sounds like he's laughing.

As soon as I'm dragged into the hallway, I rip off the bird's head and gasp for air.

Chris holds me steady. "You okay, Rae?"

"Just get me out of this thing!"

Becca bursts through the auditorium door. "Rae, are you okay? That was insane!"

I grunt as I step out of the costume. "Those little shits attacked me. If I didn't know any better, I'd think Jax planned it."

"Who planned it?" Chris asks.

"No one. Never mind."

Becca hands me a water bottle. "Drink this. I'll take your class back to my room and put on a movie. You should get checked by the nurse."

I shake my head. "I'm fine. The costume's pretty thick."

"Are you sure? You didn't hit your head?"

"Nothing but a bruised ego."

"You're tough," Chris says with a smile. "It's gonna take a lot more than a few third graders to take you down."

His comment sparks an idea. A smile spreads across my face. "You know what, Chris? I think you're right."

"Uh-oh," Becca says. "I don't like that look."

CHAPTER TWELVE

Days Left Until Summer Break: 178
Jaxon

I haven't been able to stop smiling since yesterday.

All I wanted was for Raegan to wear the mascot costume. Just a few minutes of humiliation and torture was all I'd asked for. But once again, the universe handed me a present.

The video of Raegan getting pummeled by nine-year olds went viral. Hats off to whichever teacher uploaded it to YouTube. I've already watched it thirteen times. My only regret is that I couldn't see Raegan's face while she was on the floor inside that ridiculous costume.

That's what we call karma, ladies and gentlemen.

It's eight-thirty and my second day as principal is about to start. As soon as I settle into my chair, there's a knock at the door.

"Come in."

Raegan's smiling face pokes through the doorway. I despise the lying thief, but my dick doesn't seem to have received the memo. Raegan is wearing a pale blue dress that hugs her curves in all the right spots. Her heels accentuate her toned legs, and it takes all my power to block the image of those legs wrapped around my neck when ...

She stole Nana's ring. Remember that.

Eyes on the prize, not on her thighs.

I clear my throat and adjust my pants under the desk. "Good Morning, Raegan. Glad to see you're alive and well after yesterday's fiasco."

She strides toward me and places a Starbucks cup on my desk. "Oh, that was nothing."

I raise my eyebrows. "Really? Because it looked like you took a few good hits while you were down there on the floor."

Her jaw works under her skin and I know I've gotten to her. "It's going to take a lot more than that to take me down."

Double entendre much? I gesture to the plastic cup in front of me. "What's this?"

"You helped me yesterday, and I helped you. We're even now. Take this iced coffee as an olive branch." She lifts her own cup and slips the straw between her bowed lips for a sip.

Stop looking at her lips, I tell my dick. *You're not helping.*

I shake the ice in the cup and take a swig. "Funny how you think five minutes in a costume and some coffee makes us even."

"Still haven't found your grandmother's ring?"

"Still not ready to confess?"

"If that's what you're waiting for, don't hold your breath." She pauses, eyes flicking to the ceiling like she's thinking. "On second thought, maybe you *should* hold your breath." Her lips curve into a smirk before she turns and struts out of my office, leaving her scent of coconut and pineapple behind.

I mash my teeth together, anger bubbling at the surface.

Then the bell rings.

"Get your shit together, Waters." Standing, I swipe the coffee off my desk and gulp it until it's gone. Gonna need all my energy. The second day is always harder than the first.

"You came back," Beth says when I exit my office.

"Who else is going to give you your sugar fix?" I plop a paper bag onto her desk and watch her tear into it with wide eyes.

"Donuts? Are you trying to buy my loyalty, Mr. Waters?"

"Is it working?"

She takes a mammoth-sized bite of the chocolate donut I bought her and smiles, crumbs falling onto her desk. "It absolutely is."

I wink and waltz out into the hallway. Students pile in through the main entrance and greet me on their way to class. Several of them high-five me.

A stabbing pain shoots through my stomach. I peek my head into the office again. "Beth, what time is my meeting this morning?"

"Nine o'clock, sir."

I turn my wrist and check my watch as I hurry to the men's bathroom. Twenty minutes is plenty of time.

By lunchtime, I've been to the bathroom a total of eight times.

Bet you saw that one coming, huh?

That little witch put something in my coffee.

Olive branch, my ass.

When the last wave of explosive diarrhea simmers down, I head to the kindergarten wing. I catch Raegan just as she's slinging her lunchbox on her shoulder. The kids have left for recess, and her friends are nowhere in sight. I've got her cornered.

She smiles when she sees me. "Enjoy your coffee this morning?"

"I did. Just came to thank you."

She leans closer, looking up at me with false innocence gleaming in her eyes. "Are you feeling okay? You look a little green."

I cage her in, pressing my palms against the whiteboard so I don't wrap them around her neck and strangle her instead. "I feel wonderful. Never better."

"Just be careful. Newbies always get sick at the start of school. Their bodies aren't used to all the germs." She reaches out and runs her fingers along my tie. "Wouldn't want to see you catch a bug or anything, sir."

"I'm touched at your concern for my health, Ms. Donahue."

"Just looking out for our amazing new principal."

Her words are laced with venom. My gaze lowers, taking in her heaving chest, her satin skin, her lips less than an inch from mine. The proximity is too much. I need to get away from her. Get her out of my head. I drop my hands and stalk out of the room.

I'm going to get her back. Two can play at this game. And I'm going to hit back twice as hard.

CHAPTER THIRTEEN

Raegan

"*H*e ran to that bathroom like a bear was chasing him. I wish you could've seen him!"

The girls and I are eating lunch, laughing about my successful laxative prank. Andrea caught Jaxon in a mad dash to the restroom this morning, and she has reenacted it several times. My stomach muscles ache from laughing so hard.

"I can't believe he actually drank it," Sammi says. "That's one of the oldest tricks in the book."

"Guess he's not as smart as he thinks he is." I flip my hair over my shoulder and grin.

Becca shakes her head. "I don't like this, Rae. This tit-for-tat game is only going to get worse. Who knows what that man is capable of?"

"She's not wrong," Mary says. "I'd hate to see you lose your job over this petty bullshit."

"I just wanted to send him a message." I stab the air with my index finger. "I've been pushed around for too long. If I wanted to be mistreated, I would've stayed with Andrew. I will not let Jaxon walk all over me."

"Atta girl." Kerry slaps her palm against mine.

"You're playing with fire," Becca warns. "Just be careful."

The truth is, I'm just as nervous as Becca. Though I have tenure, which makes firing me a difficult task, Jaxon still holds a lot of power over me. He could send me to another school in our district if he wanted to. I'd lose my friends and the familiarity of a school I've worked in for eight years. Things could get a lot worse.

But ever since my divorce, I've had a surge of my own power. I've wasted too much time letting a man control me. Too much time being belittled and humiliated. I can't allow Jaxon to think I'm going to roll over and let him disrespect me. When you give a man an inch, they'll come for everything else you've got until you're left with nothing.

I won't let that happen to me again.

At the end of the day, I wave goodbye to my last student. Twisting my hair into a top knot and switching from my heels to my flip-flops, I straighten up the classroom.

Joshua's second day was tear-free. He and Hannah were glued to each other's sides, and Jaxon is to thank for that. I hate to admit it, but I have to give credit where credit is due.

After I put the chairs up on the desks, I return to my own desk. Teachers never get to enjoy sitting at their desks. It's the dumping ground for important papers that never get filed away in their respective homes. Mine looks like a tornado blew through the room, but I don't have the energy to touch it right now.

On top of the mess, a colorful paper catches my eye. It's a card addressed to Jaxon from Joshua. His kid spelling is quite good for a kindergartener. I smile as I read it. He's thanking his principal for helping him on his first day at school.

For the first time, I wonder what Jaxon's family said about the missing ring. Did he cry when his grandmother passed? Was he close with her? How must it feel to have lost such an important family heirloom?

I might've made him shit his brains out today, but I still have a heart.

I could be a jerk and throw out the picture, but I can't bring myself to do that to Joshua. Instead, I swallow my pride and walk down to Jaxon's office.

His door is open and for just a moment, I allow myself to enjoy the sight of him without his nasty attitude ruining the view. His suit jacket is draped over the back of his chair. The sleeves of his grey dress shirt are rolled up, revealing his tan, muscular forearms. His jaw is clenched, and a thick crease sits between his dark brows.

It's a shame. He looks beautiful when he's not being such a jerk.

"Whatcha lookin' at, Rae?"

I jump almost a foot off the ground at the sound of Beth's voice. "Jesus H. Christ! You scared me!"

"I'd be scared too if I got caught ogling the new principal." She wiggles her eyebrows at me.

I roll my eyes and feign ignorance. "I was not ogling him. I just ... didn't want to disturb him. He looks busy."

She flashes me a knowing smile before turning her attention back to the computer. "He's definitely stressed, but I'm sure a pretty thing like you could cheer him right up."

"Don't be ridiculous."

"Why is that ridiculous? You're divorced now, aren't ya?"

"That's not the point." I lower my voice. "He's a jerk."

Her eyebrows lift as she turns to face me. "That man? Tall, dark, and Prince Charming?"

I nod. "Big, fat, jerk."

"I can't even picture it."

I cross my arms over my chest. "He's giving you chocolate, isn't he?"

She averts her eyes and starts typing on her keyboard. "I don't know what you're talking about."

"I'm so disappointed in you, Beth."

I'm only joking, and she knows it. Beth has had my back since my first day of my first year at Roosevelt Elementary. Not everybody in our school treats our secretary with the respect she deserves, and it's a shame. She's fiercely loyal and works harder than anyone I've ever known. This school would not survive without her.

I turn toward Jaxon's office once again. He spots me before I lift my hand to knock.

Scrubbing his hand over his jaw, he says, "I don't have time for whatever this is about, Raegan."

I wave Joshua's picture like a white flag as I enter his office. "I didn't come to argue. I just wanted you to have this."

He snatches the paper from my hand, but his expression softens as soon as he realizes what it is.

Without saying anything else, I turn to leave.

"Wait."

I face him again and hold my breath, ready to absorb whatever he fires at me.

"Thank you for bringing this to me." His eyes are sincere as they look into mine.

My guard lowers, just a little. "I figured you might need something to remind you of why you took this job."

We remain in silence, staring into each other's eyes. For a small moment, it's like we're not at odds with each other. For a small moment, I'm reminded why I'd felt attracted to him the first night we met.

Then his gaze drops and his hard mask returns. The moment is gone. "You can leave now. I have a lot of work to do."

For the first time all week, I leave school feeling lighter. The almost-civil exchange between me and Jaxon shifted my thinking. If I can continue to play to his softer side, things might not be so bad.

CHAPTER FOURTEEN

Days Left Until Summer Break: 177
Jaxon

Mission: Take Raegan Down is under way.

I might've had the Hershey squirts all day yesterday, but today is a new day. The ball's in my court now. Literally *and* figuratively speaking.

I tack the sign-up sheet to the bulletin board in the main office and stand back to admire the next phase of my plan.

Beth sits on the edge of her desk and raises an eyebrow. "That the sign-up for the game next month?"

"It is. Are you interested in playing?"

She shakes her head with force. "That's a brute sport."

"Ah, come on. It's all in good fun. It's for charity."

"Every year, that's what the principals say. And every year, someone leaves on a stretcher."

I return to my office so she can't see my smirk. I know exactly what happens at the game each year, and I'm looking forward to it.

Two minutes later, Raegan and her posse enter the main office right on schedule. I sit back and wait for it.

Showtime in three ...

Two ...

One.

Raegan marches into my office without knocking. She's in another dress today, this one a crimson red—matching the current color of her cheeks.

"Good Morning, Ms. Donahue."

Her hand flies up to stop the pleasantries. "You cannot sign me up for a voluntary sporting event."

I rock back in my chair, twirling a pen with my fingers. "As your principal, I can do whatever I want."

She balls her fists at her sides. "You can't treat me this way. I didn't do anything wrong."

I shrug, knowing my calm demeanor is only stoking her anger. "I'm calling on your school spirit."

"And I'm calling bullshit."

"You can put a stop to this, you know."

She steps forward and places her palms on my desk, speaking through gritted teeth. "I didn't steal that fucking ring."

I lean in, resting my weight on my elbows. "Then I guess you're playing in that fucking game."

A strangled noise escapes her throat as she leaves in a fury of blond hair and clacking heels.

I must be a special brand of fucked up, because I watch Raegan's ass bounce away until she's out of sight, totally unfazed by the fact that I just forced a woman into playing dodgeball.

I'VE BEEN OUT OF MY OFFICE FOR MOST OF THE DAY. THERE MUST BE a full moon coming tonight because the kids in this school are feral. I've had to sign off on six conduct reports and three incident reports.

At one o'clock, I fall into my comfy rolling chair behind my desk. My door is closed, and I'm hoping to catch up on e-mails and make a dent in this paperwork piled high on my desk.

I place my hand on my mousepad, feeling around for the mouse.

What the ...?

Where's the damn mouse?

I check under my desk and inside the drawers, but it doesn't take too long for realization to set in.

"Goddamnit."

I tear open the door and stomp down the hallway.

Raegan's at the whiteboard in her classroom in the middle of a math lesson. She doesn't look surprised when I barge into her room and start searching through the drawers in her desk.

She does, however, look like a cat who's been caught with a mouthful of bird.

With a bounce in her step, she waltzes over to me. "Good Afternoon, Principal Waters. Can I help you? What is it that you're looking for?"

Glancing at the class briefly, I give her a hard stare and smile. "You know exactly what I'm looking for."

"I can assure you that I don't."

I edge closer to her, lowering my lips to her ear. Her warm, sweet scent wafts into my nostrils, and I fight the urge to run my nose along her neck. *Focus, Waters. Jesus.* "Give it back, or things are going to get a lot worse for you around here."

Her eyes blaze as they lock with mine. She closes the gap between us, her chest almost pressed flush against me, and she whispers, "You don't scare me."

A shiver racks through my body. I can't decide if I want to strangle her or fuck her right here on her desk. I'm starting to gain a better understanding of people who have a choking fetish.

"Hi, Principal Waters!" Hannah's waving at me with Joshua at her side.

I clear my throat and straighten my tie. "Hi, Hannah. Hello, class. I hope you're all having a great day full of fun and learning."

Raegan chokes back a laugh as she saunters back to the whiteboard.

Laugh it up now. You won't be laughing for much longer.

THE REST OF SEPTEMBER GOES ON LIKE A TENNIS MATCH.

Or more like a fucked up, sabotage-filled, immature version of a tennis match.

After Raegan's little stunt, I started locking my office door. Fool me once, lesson learned.

But she's found other ways to get back at me.

During a faculty meeting one afternoon, Raegan "accidentally" spilled her coffee on my crotch. If you're wondering whether it was hot or iced coffee, you must be a woman. A man would know that either temperature means equally bad news for the prized possession in my pants.

Iced. It was iced.

So what did I do to retaliate?

I tripped her on her way out of the meeting. Legit stuck my foot out in front of her and tripped her.

It's a shame our gym teacher, Chris, was there to catch her.

The next week was especially fun. You can hear the sarcasm dripping from my voice when I say that, right?

I'd received a page over the loudspeaker stating that there was an emergency in Room 1. I should've known it was another one of Raegan's pranks, but I reacted on instinct. I sprinted down the hall and burst through the classroom door to find Raegan and her students sitting calmly at the carpet.

"What's the emergency?" I asked, out of breath.

"Did Beth page *you*? Oh, I'm sorry. I meant to call for the custodian. Jayden here had an accident on our floor."

I looked down and found myself standing in a heaping pile of Jayden's shit.

Allow me to reiterate that: The kid pulled his pants down in the middle of the classroom and took a dump on the tile floor the way a bear shits in the woods.

And then I stepped in it.

You're probably wondering what I did after that.

I laughed.

I *laughed*.

I hear that's a sign of insanity.

By the end of the month, I was fresh out of ideas. I spent way too much of my time on YouTube watching prank videos. And let me tell you, the things kids come up with are scary. No one is safe. Kids these days are nuts.

Anyway, I snuck into Raegan's classroom and removed what looked like an important screw from her chair.

Unfortunately, I wasn't able to witness her falling flat on her ass when the chair gave out, but I caught her rubbing her back later on. That was enough for me. I'm not greedy.

I have to hand it to her. Raegan's been winning the little battles. And that's okay. Honestly, it is.

Because I know I'm going to win the war.

CHAPTER FIFTEEN

Days Left Until Summer Break: 162
Raegan

"*I* can't believe you're going through with this."

Staring at my reflection in the mirror, I puff out my chest and clench my fists. "I'm going to make Principal Fuckwad regret signing me up for this game."

Becca plants her hand on her hip, balancing William on the other. "You remember what happened to Tanya last year, right?"

"Two black eyes and a broken nose. Let's hope Fuckwad doesn't have good aim."

Mia runs around me in circles. "Fuckwad! Fuckwad! Fuckwad!"

Becca covers her face with her hand. "It took me a week to get them to stop shouting *sex* every time we went to Shoprite."

"I just gave her a new word to fixate on. You're welcome."

She flips me off in the mirror.

I wrap the hair tie one more time around my ponytail and pull to tighten it. I'm wearing a black T-shirt with the school logo on the front and a pair of black running shorts. I bought black knee-high socks and to complete the sporty look, I painted black lines under my eyes.

On the outside, I appear tough and ready for battle.

On the inside, I'm shaking like a leaf on a tree in the middle of winter, barely holding on.

I played soccer when I was a kid, but that's nothing compared to a contact sport like dodgeball.

Could I have told Jaxon that I wasn't going to play? Sure. I could get in my car right now and go home. Principals can't force teachers to volunteer.

But that would make me appear weak. Afraid. I want Jaxon to know that I won't cower, I won't be bullied.

Plus, how could I pass up the chance to launch a ball at his stupid, handsome face?

Becca peeks in the back end of William's diaper. "Again, dude? Seriously? Why don't you ever poop when Daddy's around?"

Mia stares up at me, pinching her nose with her tiny fingers. "He smells."

I kneel in front of her. "When are *you* going to poop on the potty, little miss?"

She throws her hands in the air and screams, "Never!"

I laugh. "You tell Mommy that she may take your life, but she will never take your diapers!" I take off running down the hallway with Mia right behind me. "Freedom!"

"Not helping, Braveheart," Becca calls.

Sure, *that* movie reference she gets.

When we get to the living room, I lift Mia and swing her in a circle before tossing her onto the couch. "Seriously, girl. What's it gonna take for you to poop on the big girl potty?"

"I want a pony."

I flop down next to her. "If you think William's poop smells, wait until you smell the poop from a pony." I wave my hand in front of my nose for effect.

"Eww." She scrunches her nose. "I want a kitty instead."

Now it's my turn to scrunch my face in disgust. "Kitties are evil little creatures."

Mia's eyes are saucers. "Really?"

"It's true. They'll eat your body when you die in your apartment, single and alone. What kind of loyalty is that?"

Her bottom lip trembles. "I don't want the kitty to eat me."

"Thank you for the nightmares she's going to have tonight," Becca says, sitting on the recliner with a clean-bottomed William.

"She doesn't want ponies or cats anymore, so I did you a solid." I turn my attention back to the brown-eyed girl climbing into my lap. "What about toys, Mia? Anything you really want?"

"I want a pink Barbie car!"

"That I can do. If you start going peepee and poopie on the potty, I'll get you that Barbie car."

"Yay!" Mia kicks her feet. "I'm getting a Barbie car. I'm getting a Barbie car."

"She's gonna hold you to that, you know," Becca says. "Kid has the memory of an elephant."

"Let me know how she does in her big girl underwear and I'll have that car here by next week." I stand and stretch my arms overhead.

Mia stands on the couch cushion. "Where are you going?"

"Your Auntie Rae Rae is about to lay the smack down on someone." I flex my bicep and wiggle my eyebrows.

"I want to lay the smack down! Can I go, Mommy?"

"No, babe. We're going to stay here and wait for Aunt Rae to call us from the hospital."

I glare at Becca. "You have no faith in me. I will *not* be going to the hospital."

At least I hope not.

"Rae, you look badass!"

I grimace at Kerry and Andrea. "I'm starting to get nervous."

Kerry shakes me by my shoulders. "You've got this. You're the toughest chick I know."

"I am?"

"No, but you're tougher than Sammi so that counts for something."

My shoulders slump. "Is he here yet?"

"Haven't seen him." Kerry pulls something out of her purse and hands it to me. "Put this on."

My eyes widen as I take the plastic mouth guard from her. "You really think I'll need this?"

"Better safe than sorry. You don't want to get your teeth knocked out, do you?"

My stomach flops and I groan.

Andrea laughs and shakes her head. "Rae, you're going to be fine. All you had to do was show up tonight. You don't have to win the entire game. Just show Principal Fuckwad who he's messing with."

"Raegan, come on!" Chris waves me over to the rest of my team.

I nod and take one last look at my friends. "Thanks for coming, guys. I'll see you after the game." *Hopefully*.

Bleachers line the gymnasium. Students and their parents hold up signs they've created to represent their favorite teachers. I spot Joshua in the front row. He beams when we make eye contact and waves excitedly.

No sign of Jaxon though. Maybe he isn't playing. Maybe I've been worried for nothing.

Chris wraps his arm around my shoulders. "You ready, Raegan?"

"As I'll ever be."

"You got beat up by a mob of angry students. This will be a cake walk for you."

I force a smile. "If only there was cake involved."

He squeezes me before dropping his arm and turning to the team.

My team isn't that bad. Even though we have Mrs. Gallagher, the oldest teacher in our entire district, we also have Rebecca, our computer teacher. She's tall, and I've seen her crush a beer can on her forehead at one of our holiday parties. Maybe I can hide behind her and use her as a human shield.

"Mrs. Gallagher, you and Mrs. Stevenson can hang in the back," Chris says. "I want you guys collecting the balls once they hit the floor. Rae and Michelle will stay off to the sides. You ladies are going to distract the other team. Aim low.

"Rebecca and I will be up at the front. They'll be so focused on trying to take us out, Rae and Michelle should be able to pick them off when they're not looking."

The sound of a whistle slices through the room. When I glance up, Jaxon is front and center on his side of the court.

Shit. He's here.

In a black T-shirt that stretches across his broad chest, sleeves snug around his muscular biceps, he stands tall and proud with a dazzling smile.

His good looks only make me angry. They're wasted on such an asshole.

"Thank you all for coming," his deep voice booms over the microphone. "And thank you to the teachers who volunteered to entertain everyone tonight. We're all here for a great cause. Your donation will go towards feeding the underprivileged families in our town."

My hands are shaking. *Come on, Rae. You're raising money for the kids who need it. You can do this.*

When Jaxon's speech ends, the room erupts in applause and cheers. Chris points out where he wants us to stand, and I slip my mouth guard into place. I expect Jaxon to take the spot opposite me, but he hangs back instead. I don't have time to wonder what his plan is because the whistle blows and we all rush toward the balls in the middle of the room.

Game on, Fuckwad.

CHAPTER SIXTEEN

Jaxon

*E*veryone always runs for a ball when a dodgeball game starts. Everyone but me. I wait. Watch. Look for the weak links.

It's obvious that Mrs. Gallagher and Mrs. Stevenson are the easiest targets, but Chris put them in the back. Smart strategy. He and Rebecca are going to be tough to beat.

Michelle's a new teacher. She's pale with dark hair and thick black-framed glasses. She looks like she belongs in a tech lab rather than a dodgeball game. But when you don't have tenure, you have to step up and volunteer for everything. Poor thing. She should be easy to pick off.

Then there's Raegan. I almost laughed when I saw the black streaks under her eyes, but my gaze continued downward to her legs in those tight black shorts. I remember when I tossed those legs over my shoulders and buried my face in her ...

Focus, you idiot!

Chris lobs a ball at me, but I step out of the way. As I do, another ball whizzes past my ankle from the left. It misses me, but it was a close one. And who's smiling at me from the direction that ball came from?

I'll give you one guess.

The ring thief almost got me. I crouch down and grab a ball. Rebecca fires at me but I use the ball in my hands to deflect it. I could go after Raegan now, but I want to build her confidence a little. Let her think she stands a chance. So I launch the ball at Mrs. Stevenson instead. She attempts to catch it but it bounces off her outstretched fingers. She's out. One down.

Two minutes seem like an eternity. Rebecca manages to knock two of my teammates out of the game right before the round ends. The whistle blows and the crowd cheers while the players jog to their water bottles.

When the second round starts, I stay on Raegan's side of the court. She's good at being sneaky, so I need to keep an eye on her at all times. Two of my teammates gang up on Rebecca and try to knock her out of the game. Another takes out Mrs. Gallagher.

Chris and Raegan try double-teaming me again, but that trick will only work once. I dodge Raegan's and catch the one Chris threw just as the whistle blows. Chris is out of the game, and Raegan looks like someone kicked her puppy.

In the last round, it's Raegan and Michelle against me and my VP, Mrs. Wilcox.

Perfect. We'll take out Michelle first.

At least, that's what I expect to happen when Mrs. Wilcox and I launch our balls at Michelle. Remember when I said the new teacher looks like she belongs in a tech lab? Yeah, well ... I misjudged her. She jumps over my ball and catches Mrs. Wilcox's ball in mid-air.

My VP is out. Now it's two against one. I'm the lone ranger. A sitting duck. Michelle, Raegan, and I each have a ball. I know that once I throw mine, they will throw theirs. My reflexes are good, but I need to be prepared.

I wouldn't be so worried if I wasn't playing against the jewel thief and the Michael Jordan of dodgeball.

Raegan and Michelle raise their balls in the air, winding up for simultaneous throws. When their arms come down, I throw mine at

Raegan. Hard. Harder than I should be throwing at an elementary school charity game.

But the girls fake their throws and hold onto their balls. Raegan uses hers to deflect mine, sending my own ball hurtling back at me. It slams into my face and my body jerks backward.

CHAPTER SEVENTEEN

Raegan

I just knocked out my principal.

Half of me wants to cry and the other half wants to dance around his unconscious body.

It was a total accident. All I did was deflect his ball—the ball he launched like a nuclear missile at my head. I had no control over where it bounced to.

Jaxon won't see it that way though. Then again, he might not see much if his eye keeps swelling like it is.

I kneel down beside him, my hand involuntarily reaching out to stroke his hair. "Jaxon? Can you hear me?"

Chris and our teammates keep the families calm and in their seats. Mrs. Wilcox and the rest of Jaxon's team huddle around us.

"Should we call an ambulance?" I ask.

"Let's give him a minute and see if he wakes up," Mrs. Wilcox says. "We don't want to alarm the children."

Kerry and Andrea bring over a bottle of water and a few paper towels. I use them to dab cool water on Jaxon's neck and head.

"Come on, Jaxon. Wake up," I whisper.

My fingers are still in his hair when his eyelids flutter. Just before they open, he leans into my touch. A low groan rumbles in his throat.

Shit. He must've hit his head harder than I thought. "Are ... are you okay, Jaxon? Do you know where you are?"

His eyes open and fixate on me. His lips curve into a smirk. "First you steal my ring, then you poison my coffee. Now you try to decapitate me. I'm starting to think you're an assassin, Raegan."

"I was just hoping you'd wake up with amnesia."

He chuckles. "Forget you? Not a chance."

The crowd cheers as Mrs. Wilcox and I help Jaxon to his feet. Joshua bolts off the bench and wraps his arms around Jaxon's leg. Jaxon lifts him up in a bear hug. "I'm okay, buddy. See? Nothing to worry about."

The crowd *oohs* and *aahs* over the two of them.

Jaxon takes the microphone. "Well, folks. Let's hear it for the winners of this charity game. And to all the boys out there who just witnessed their principal get beat by two girls: Don't ever underestimate a girl just because she's a girl."

Everyone cheers while Jaxon and Joshua pose for pictures.

"I have to give it to him," Kerry says. "The man is charming."

"That he is." *And of course the black eye only makes him hotter.*

While the gymnasium clears out, I turn around to Michelle. "Where did you learn to play like that?"

"I have three older brothers." She shrugs. "You get good at dodging and throwing things."

I laugh. "Is this your first year teaching?"

"It is. Hopefully I made a good impression on our principal by volunteering for this game."

"You're not the one who rendered him unconscious, so I'd say you're safe." I wink and nudge her with my elbow. "If you ever need anything, I'm in Room 1. Don't hesitate to come ask for help."

"Thanks so much. I might take you up on that. I could use a friend around here."

"Then consider us friends."

Once the building is empty, Kerry, Andrea, Michelle and I make our way toward the exit. The light streaming out of Jaxon's office catches my eye.

Maybe the adrenaline's wearing off after the game, or maybe this feud is draining me. Maybe I'm just a glutton for punishment.

"Oh, crap. I forgot my car keys in my classroom," I lie. "You guys go ahead. I'll see you tomorrow."

The girls wave, and I wait until they're out of sight before turning into the main office.

Jaxon is sifting through paperwork while holding an icepack on his right eye.

"Planning on sleeping here?" I ask, stepping slowly into his office.

He doesn't look up at me. "I was thinking about putting a cot next to the filing cabinet."

I stop at the corner of his desk. "Is your eye okay?"

"Why do you care?"

"Contrary to your belief, I'm actually a compassionate person."

"That so?"

"Plus, my mom's a nurse. Let me take a look."

I edge closer until I'm standing over him. He doesn't protest as I remove the ice pack, and he lets me tilt his chin upward so I can assess the damage in the light. His dark eyes peer up at me. It's like looking into deep, turbulent water, unsure of what's lurking beneath the surface.

"Just some bruising and swelling." I move my index finger back and forth. I have no clue what nurses are looking for when they do this, but it makes me look legit. "How's your vision?"

"I can see you perfectly." His gaze drops to my lips and his Adam's apple bobs.

The scent of his cologne surrounds me, a mixture of vanilla and mint. With his face so close to mine, I'm brought back to the night we met. Back when he was nothing more than a beautiful stranger. Before this whole mess began.

What I wouldn't give to be able to do it all over again.

"What would you do differently?" he asks.

My eyes widen. *Shit, I said that out loud.* I have to get out of here. I take a step back, followed by another, until I can no longer feel the pull between us. "Keep icing it. Take some ibuprofen when you get home. If you experience any vomiting, you should go to the hospital. That's a sign of a concussion."

He smirks. "Or too much whiskey."

I roll my eyes and turn away, making it all the way to the door before I stop. "You know what I'd do differently? I'd stay. If I never ran out of your apartment that morning, if I stayed, maybe things would be different now."

Jaxon gives me a long, unreadable look. "Guess we'll never know."

"I really am telling you the truth. I didn't steal your grandmother's ring. I'd never do something like that."

He sighs and returns his attention to the pile of papers in front of him, as if I never said anything at all.

CHAPTER EIGHTEEN

Days Left Until Summer Break: 157
Jaxon

I press snooze for the third time this morning.

Since the night of the dodgeball game, I haven't been able to sleep. I toss and turn, unable to drift off. And when I finally do, I have a dream. I wake up exhausted, out of breath, and drenched in sweat.

Something is tormenting me, gnawing at my gut.

Or more like some*one*.

It's the same dream every night. Raegan and I are fucking in my office. She's wearing a short, black dress with heels. I bend her over my desk and take her from behind. It's vivid as fuck. It's the hottest dream sex I've ever had. I wake up with a raging hard-on, but I've been too stubborn to jerk off to the woman who stole from me.

I've been taking a lot of cold showers.

This morning though ... my willpower is dwindling. I've been running on no sleep for a week. It'd drive any person to the brink of insanity. I can't be held responsible for my actions. I'm not thinking straight.

At least that's my excuse when my hand trails down my stomach and slips under the waistband of my boxers.

Try not to judge me. I need a release. I need relief.

My mind is consumed with thoughts of Raegan. I'm constantly thinking of ways to get her to confess to her crime. And when I'm not, I'm thinking of ways to lash out at her. When neither of those thoughts are at the forefront of my mind? That's when the image of her glorious, naked body in my bed enters from left field. Her legs spread open for me, hips grinding against my tongue ...

I pump my fist over my length, hard and fast in angry strokes. I don't want to draw this out. I want it over. Want to be rid of her. I don't *like* being attracted to a woman I hate. It's wrong. It's torturing me.

I think the problem is that I keep getting little glimpses of Raegan's good side. The side I'd been introduced to the night we met.

Let's go down the list.

She's good at her job and she works hard. That's sexy to me.

She brought me the picture Joshua had made for me on the second day of school. She could've thrown it out. An evil person would have. But not Raegan.

Then there's the way she caressed my head when she knew I was hurt at the dodgeball game. That wasn't the touch of someone without humanity. And the fact that she'd stopped in my office to check on me after? That blew my mind.

It's like she's two people inside one body. The beautiful, caring woman, and the closet psychopath who robs jewelry from sleeping men.

Never-ending questions continue to plague me.

What if she never gives up the ring?

What if it's gone forever?

What if ...

What if she really didn't steal it?

"HOW IS EVERYTHING GOING WITH THE GIRL?"

"Raegan," I say. I don't know why it bothers me when he refers to her like that, but it does.

Dad looks at me over the top of his glasses. "How is everything going with Raegan?"

Running my fingers along the framed family photo on Dad's bookcase, I sigh. "She's still saying she didn't take it."

"Of course she's saying that. That's what thieves do. They lie."

"Do you remember when we took this picture?" I raise the frame and face it towards Dad. "Nana was so happy when we gave it to her for Christmas."

A smile tugs at the corner of Dad's mouth. "I remember how difficult it was for you and Josh to agree on which color shirt to wear."

My eyes flick to another photo sitting on a different shelf. A five-year old me is holding a two-year old Josh in my lap. "Were we always so opposite?"

"Always."

"It's crazy how that happens. Two boys with the same family and same upbringing. How can we be so different?"

Dad slips his glasses off and sets them on his desk. "It's just the way you're born. I know the whole Michaela thing didn't help."

I return the frame back to the bookshelf and settle into the chair facing Dad's desk. "I don't know what else to do."

"About the girl?"

"Yes. About Raegan."

Dad tilts back in his chair, appraising me, arms crossed over his chest. "What do you want to do?"

"I've tried making her life miserable at work. I've tried intimidation. I've tried being nice." I hike a shoulder. "What if I never get Nana's ring back?"

He puffs up his cheeks and blows a stream of air through his lips. "I spoke to Harry at work. He said his brother-in-law is a police officer. He could try to get us a search warrant."

My eyebrows shoot up. "And search her house?"

"She's a public employee. We can get her address. If she has the ring, they'll find it."

"What if she already pawned it?"

"Harry's been keeping an eye on the local places. So far, nobody's seen the ring."

The door to Dad's office flies open. Josh closes it behind him and rushes toward me. "You *lost* Nana's ring?"

I push out of the chair to face him. "You were eavesdropping?"

He scoffs. "The walls are thin. I was walking out of the bathroom when I heard Dad talking about pawn shops." He shakes his head. "I can't believe you lost it."

Dad's voice booms. "Josh, sit down. You don't know what you're talking about."

"You're going to defend him? Nana left the ring to him and he lost it." He looks me up and down, his top lip curling. "So much for being the better choice."

I step toward him so that we're almost nose to nose. There's a slight height difference between us and I use it to my advantage. "Like it would've been in better hands with you? It would've ended up in a pawn shop before the end of the day."

"You can't hold onto anything these days can you? First your girlfriend, now the ring."

I fist Josh's T-shirt in my hands and slam him against the bookcase. "You piece of shit—"

"Enough!" Dad's fist slams onto the desk. He stands, his voice low and intimidating as he points to the door. "Get out, both of you."

I release Josh's shirt and shove my hands through my hair. With our tails tucked between our legs, we leave Dad's office.

Mom's waiting in the hallway, her eyes darting from Josh to me. "Boys, what's going on?"

I place my hand on her shoulder and muster a smile. "Nothing, Mom. Everything's fine."

She sighs. "Then get out of this hallway and let's go eat dinner."

Josh wraps his arm around her waist. "Smells great. Let's go." As they walk toward the kitchen, Josh turns and smirks at me over his shoulder.

CHAPTER NINETEEN

Days Left Until Summer Break: 155
Raegan

"For the final order of business, we have Halloween coming up."

Every teacher in the room groans.

Jaxon laughs and holds his hands up. "Don't shoot the messenger. I'm putting a sign-up sheet in the main office for anyone who would like to volunteer to help with the dance. Whether you can chaperone or decorate, your help will be greatly appreciated. I know it's an exhausting day for you guys, but try to remember who we're doing this for."

I raise my hand and Jaxon points to me. "There are a lot of students whose families can't afford costumes. Maybe we can set up a donation box by the front door. The staff and parents can donate old costumes for any families that can't afford to buy them."

I expect him to shoot me down, but Jaxon's face breaks into a wide smile. "That is a fantastic idea. Great job, Raegan."

I almost fall out of my chair from sheer shock.

Jaxon's gaze sweeps around the room. "If nobody has anything else they'd like to add, you can all go home."

Becca nudges me as we stand. "I think you knocked something loose when you hit him with that ball."

"I don't know, but I'm not buying the nice guy act."

"You don't have to buy it. Just enjoy it."

I spot Michelle walking ahead of us in the hallway. "Hey, Michelle! Wait up."

She spins around and smiles. "Hey. I was just on my way to sign up to chaperone at the Halloween dance. Are you guys volunteering?"

"I'll do it with you." I gesture to my friends. "The girls have their own kids to take Trick-or-Treating so I'll be riding solo."

"Have fun," Kerry says. "I'd rather gouge my eyes out with a rusty spoon than stay here for two more hours for that dance."

I shove her. "Don't listen to her, Michelle. She's becoming one of those old teachers who doesn't remember how to find the fun anymore."

Kerry flips me off before heading down the kindergarten wing.

"Do you mind signing my name for me?" Michelle asks. "I have ten minutes to get across town to make it for a dentist appointment."

"Sure thing. See you tomorrow."

In the main office, Beth is sitting at her desk, licking her fingers.

I lean in and sniff her breath. "Peanut butter cups?"

She just grins.

Jaxon breezes past us on the way into his office. "I have more if you want some."

I follow him and lean my hip against his doorframe. "You're going to give her diabetes, you know."

He chuckles. "I like to keep my staff happy."

"That has yet to be seen," I mutter. "Where's the sign-up sheet? Michelle and I want to chaperone the Halloween dance."

His eyebrows shoot up. "Really? I thought I'd have to bribe and beg people to go to that thing."

"I'm not opposed to begging."

Amusement dances in Jaxon's eyes. "I'll get on my hands and knees if I have to."

I roll my eyes. "That I'd like to see."

He slides the sign-up sheet toward me, wearing that confident, flirty smirk. "Name the time and place, Ms. Donahue."

I squirm under his unwavering gaze, unable to form a witty retort. Is he flirting with me? *What's happening right now?*

I click my pen and sign both of our names at the top of the sign-up sheet. Then I high-tail it out of Jaxon's office without another word.

"HI, GRANDMA. IT'S ME, RAEGAN. YOUR GRANDDAUGHTER."

Grandma's face twists as she scoffs. "I know who you are. You don't have to introduce yourself to me, baby."

I let out the breath I've been holding, relieved that today seems to be a good day.

I never know what kind of mood Grandma will be in until I arrive in her room at the nursing home. Some days she's tired and sleeps throughout my visit. Other times she's angry and combative. It's easier when I have my mom with me, but Mom got called to do a double at the hospital, so it's just me.

I wrap my arms around my grandmother and squeeze her thin body. "How are you feeling today?"

"I'm fine. My knee hurts a bit but nothing out of the ordinary."

"That knee is still bothering you, huh? Maybe we should call the doctor to take a look at it again."

She waves her hand. "Oh, no. It's fine. Just a little bruised. Nothing to make a fuss over."

I chew on my bottom lip. "I don't like that it's still hurting you. I know you fell, but that was weeks ago."

"I'm fine, baby. Now help your grandmother up, will you? It's almost time for my therapy session."

I hold Grandma steady as she changes into her bathing suit, and then we ride the elevator down to the indoor pool.

Her physical therapist, Neil, is waiting for us once we arrive. A warm blast of chlorine-scented air burns my nostrils. I end up leaving with a headache every week, but I wouldn't miss the chance to see my grandmother's face light up when she gets into the water. She and my grandfather had a huge inground pool where I'd spend hours swimming every day as a kid. Grandma loves the water, and it's the only place she seems at peace.

Normally I wear a one-piece bathing suit with a T-shirt over it. But since I've lost the divorce weight, as I'm referring to it, I'm able to fit into my old bikinis again.

Hello, two-piece, my old friend.

I strip out of my clothes and leave them folded neatly on a chair. Taking Grandma's arm, I lead her into the pool.

Neil whistles as he reaches out for Grandma's hand. "Look at you, girl. Glad to see you ditched the baggy T-shirt. Let me find out you've been hiding that body under there the whole time."

I giggle. "More like this body was hiding under a layer of fat."

"Well, good for you for losing the weight *and* the dead weight, if you know what I'm talking about."

Neil's my favorite therapist here at Grandma's nursing home. The other ones are fine, but Grandma's happiest when she's around Neil's upbeat personality. I am too.

"My Raegan is single now," Grandma says matter-of-factly. "Maybe you'd be interested in taking her on a date."

"Gran, I don't think I'm Neil's type."

"Nonsense," she says, splashing water at me. "Neil, are you only allowed to date Egyptian women? Or are you one of those boys who likes the stick-thin model types?"

Neil and I exchange knowing smiles. "Oh, I *am* a fan of the sticks." He wiggles his eyebrows.

I do my best to suppress my laughter, but the confused look on Grandma's face is priceless.

Neil and I take my grandmother through her exercises for the next half-hour. I'm thankful to be here while she's having such a good day. I have to take what I can get, because I never know when the tides will turn.

"How's work, Rae?" Grandma asks.

"It's great. Counting down the days until Thanksgiving break. I could use a couple days off."

"Nothing like the slaughtering of the indigenous people to get everyone excited," Neil says. "Please tell me you don't still teach those kids about the Pilgrims and the Native Americans sharing a peaceful meal together."

"They're only five. I can't exactly tell them about how the Native Americans were raped and pillaged."

Neil sighs. "I get that, I suppose." He glances over the top of my head and a grin spreads across his face. "Now *that* right there is my type."

I look over my shoulder as discreetly as I can, following Neil's gaze. Then my entire body stills in the water.

Jaxon's standing at the edge of the steps, guiding an older man into the pool. His black swim trunks sit low on his hips—Jaxon's, not the old man's. No suit. No tie. His upper body is completely bare.

My eyes blaze a trail up his chiseled abdomen, over his smooth, broad chest, around the striations in his shoulders. *How could I not remember seeing* this *the night we met?* Stupid whiskey shots.

Neil chuckles. "He's so sexy, he rendered you speechless."

"That's my *boss*," I whisper-yell, unable to tear my eyes away.

"Your boss?" Neil's head whips back and forth between Jaxon and me. "Oh, honey, that man can order me around any day."

"I don't want him to see me. You have to help me get out of here."

"Oh, look," Grandma says, raising her hand to wave. "There's Samuel Waters."

It takes all my strength not to push my grandmother's head under the water and hold her there until she stops waving at Jaxon's grandfather. *Memory's working just fine today, huh?*

"Too late," Neil whispers. "He's already spotted you."

I groan and lower myself further into the water until all that's left above the surface is my head.

Jaxon and his grandfather are swimming over to us in the middle of the pool. And Jaxon's wearing that evil smirk he loves to taunt me with.

"You look like a blond Oompa Loompa minus the spray tan. Get up," Neil says, pulling my arm until I'm standing again.

I shoot him a dirty look as Jaxon and Samuel arrive.

"Hi, Raegan."

I plaster on a fake smile. "Hi, Jaxon. Didn't realize our grandparents were at the same nursing home. I've never seen you here before."

"I usually don't come on the weekends, but I've been working so late during the week that I had to switch my visits."

His grandfather nudges him with his elbow and signs something with his hands. To my surprise, Jaxon signs back. I watch their hand gestures go back and forth. Then Samuel extends his hand toward me and smiles.

I shake his hand and look up at Jaxon. "How do I sign *nice to meet you?*"

Jaxon's eyes widen and his lips part, as if he's caught off-guard by my question. He blinks a few times and clears his throat before he speaks. "Uh ... okay. First you're going to put your palms together, like this." He places one hand on top of the other. "Then you swipe your top hand over the bottom. That means *nice.*"

"Okay, so I'm making a sandwich, and then sliding it over to you," I say, mimicking his hand movements.

He laughs. "Good. Then you're going to hold both hands up like you're showing the number one. Face them towards each other, and now you have *meet.*"

"I get it. The two fingers look like they're two people meeting." I turn to Samuel and repeat the steps Jaxon showed me.

Samuel's face lights up and he claps. Then he signs something else.

"He said *good job*."

I smile and offer him the sign for *thank you*, which is the only thing I know how to sign, thanks to watching *Sesame Street* with Mia and William.

"How do you two know each other?" Grandma asks.

"We work together. Jaxon's the new principal at my school."

I watch as Jaxon's hands move to interpret for his grandfather. Samuel then signs something that makes Jaxon laugh.

"What did he say?" I ask.

"He said you're very pretty."

Heat burns my cheeks. "Thank you. Jaxon, this is my grandmother, Annette."

Jaxon shakes Grandma's hand and brings it to his lips, pressing a chaste kiss to the back of her hand. "It's a pleasure to meet you, Annette."

She fans herself. "Oh, my. What a gentleman your grandson is, Sam."

Sam watches her lips as she talks, then puffs his chest out and grins.

Jaxon points to his bruised eye. "Would you believe your grand-daughter gave me this shiner?"

Both Grandma and Neil's mouths fall open. "Well, I suspect you deserved it if that's true," Grandma says.

I laugh and wrap my arm around her shoulders. "Damn straight he deserved it."

Samuel grins as he signs.

Jaxon shakes his head, smiling. "He said he likes you, Raegan. You've got spunk."

"She gets that from me," Grandma says.

I giggle. "Tell him I like him much more than his grandson."

Jaxon clutches his chest. "That hurt."

I roll my eyes. "Well, we were just about to leave. Enjoy your swim time."

Jaxon winks. "See you on Monday, Ms. Donahue."

I wave good bye to Samuel, and swim to the steps. Grandma takes my hand and leans on Neil for support as we help her out of the pool.

"Your boss is totally checking you out," Neil whispers.

I wrap Grandma in a towel. "He is not."

"Hand to God, he hasn't taken his eyes off you since you got out of the pool."

"Raegan, that boy is very charming." Grandma touches her hand to my cheek. "Much nicer than that loser, Andrew."

"He's not as nice as he seems," I murmur.

I'm about to wrap my towel around my body, but think better of it. Jaxon wants to play games? Fine. *Eat your heart out, Fuckwad.*

I sling the towel over my arm and strut past Jaxon with my head held high.

I don't think about him for the rest of the day.

Not one single thought.

Not about how adorable he looked signing with his grandfather.

Or about how ridiculously hot he looked without a shirt on.

Not even about the way the water droplets ran down his tan, toned body ...

Okay, who am I kidding? That's all I thought about.

There's definitely something wrong with me.

CHAPTER TWENTY

Days Left Until Summer Break: 153
Jaxon

Seeing Raegan dripping wet in that turquoise bikini has done *nothing* to help my sex dreams.

Not dreams.

Nightmares.

They're nightmares. Let's get that straight.

At least that's what I keep telling myself.

Fantasizing about Raegan is the last thing I need on top of all the stress at work. It's after three-thirty. School's over, yet I'll likely be in this office until after the sun goes down. Again.

I glance out the window when a flash of blond hair catches my eye. Raegan's sitting on the bench outside with a little girl.

What's she still doing here? I throw on my jacket and exit through the double doors.

Outside my stride screeches to a halt. Raegan's hand is up, and she's moving her fingers in different positions. Her student, a girl named Peyton, lifts her hand to copy what Raegan did.

Raegan is teaching her Sign Language.

I stand there, watching in awe, until Raegan spots me. She drops her hand into her lap and smiles.

I walk toward the bench. "Ms. Donahue, is everything okay?"

"Peyton's mom is running a little late. I'm keeping her company until she gets here."

"Did Beth call her mother?"

"No, I did. I told Beth that I'd handle it. It was time for her to go home for the day."

Always worrying about others. I remove my jacket and wrap it around Raegan's shoulders. "Peyton, you should tell your teacher how important it is to wear a jacket now that it's getting colder."

Peyton's eyes widen as she nods. "Yes, Mr. Waters."

Raegan smirks. "I'm fine. I don't mind the fall weather. It's actually my favorite season."

"Mine too," says Peyton. "Do you like to jump in the leaves?"

Raegan smiles. "No, but I used to when I was your age."

"How come you don't do it anymore? Is it because you're a grown up?"

"I guess adults don't do the fun things kids get to do."

Peyton turns to me. "Do you jump in the leaves, Mr. Waters?"

I puff my chest out. "Of course I do."

"You do?" both Raegan and Peyton ask.

I look around the bench and spot a decent pile of leaves. "How about *that* pile? Want to go jump in it, Peyton?"

Her eyes light up. "Yes!" She takes my hand and pulls me onto the grass.

"On the count of three." I squat down low beside Peyton. "One, two, three!"

We dive into the pile and Peyton's squeals fills the air. We roll out of the leaves and stand. I help Peyton brush the leaf bits off her jacket. Then a silver Honda pulls to a stop in front of us and Peyton bolts to the passenger door.

"I see you're having fun," Peyton's mom says through her open window.

"Yeah, Mom. Mr. Waters is the coolest principal ever."

My chest squeezes. *I love this job.* I wave as they drive off.

"You really are something else, you know that?" Raegan says, standing and walking toward me.

"Something else? I suppose I've been called worse."

"Oh, you should hear the names I've come up with in my head."

I can't fight the smile that tugs at my mouth. "Sounds like you spend a lot of time thinking about me."

She rolls her eyes. "You *would* hear it that way."

"Were you ... were you doing Sign Language before I came outside?"

Her cheeks turn a deeper shade of pink. "I was just showing Peyton what I've learned."

"You've been learning how to sign?"

"Kerry has been teaching me. I figured I could communicate with your grandfather the next time I visited my grandma."

An odd sensation stirs in my chest. *She's learning Sign Language for my grandfather.* I can't form coherent words. I'm overcome with ... with what, exactly? No one's ever done something like that for him. For *me*.

Silence descends while we stare at one another.

Raegan is so insanely beautiful. Her nose and cheeks are rosy from the chill in the air. My jacket swallows her body, making her look even smaller than usual. I'm tempted to reach out and run my fingers through her silky blond waves, brush my lips against hers.

And the way Raegan's gaze keeps finding its way to my lips tells me she might want me to.

Raegan steps closer to me, and I lean in on instinct. I'm powerless, stuck in the gravitational pull of her green eyes. Why do I have to be so damn attracted to her? Am I that weak of a man? My body is at war with my mind, both of them pulling me in opposite directions.

Raegan stretches onto her toes, and my heart slams against my chest. She reaches up ... to pick a leaf out of my hair. Then she slips off my jacket and hands it back to me.

"Have a good night, Jaxon."

I say nothing, rooted to the ground, watching her walk into the parking lot.

Wondering what the hell just happened.

"I CAN'T BELIEVE YOU DRANK THE COFFEE! THAT'S LIKE THE OLDEST trick in the book."

I glare at Dan across the table. I'm with the guys for a much-needed happy hour, and I just filled them in on what's been going on with Raegan.

Dan clutches his stomach as he doubles over. "That girl is a genius."

I rub my temples in small circles. "And the craziest part of this whole thing? My gut keeps telling me that Raegan's telling the truth. But if that's true, then what happened to the ring?" I take a long swig from my beer bottle. "It had to be her, right?"

Smith shrugs. "Maybe this is why she's divorced. She's a nut bag."

"She might be a kleptomaniac," Shaun says. "If that's the case, it's a disease and she can't help it."

"You said she has a group of friends." Smith's eyes narrow. "Have you tried talking to them?"

My eyebrows lift. "Would you guys rat me out if I stole something?"

"No, but girls aren't always tight-lipped about things. Maybe one of them will slip and give you a clue."

"What about other co-workers? People who've worked with her for a long time but don't necessarily have allegiance to her?" Dan asks, finally recovered from his laughing fit.

I ponder that while I drain the rest of my beer. "She seems pretty chummy with the gym teacher."

"I bet your brother is having a field day with this," Shaun says.

I roll my eyes. "He's acting like all his years of immature bullshit got wiped clean. Like suddenly he's a good guy."

"What about your dad?"

"He's disappointed in me."

Dan grimaces. "That's the worst. I'd rather my old man yell at me than say he's disappointed."

"This will all blow over eventually." Smith pats me on the back. "You can't dwell on it forever. If the ring is gone, it's gone. Nothing you can do."

Shaun leans in. "What if you've been going about this all wrong? What if you pull the ultimate prank?"

I lift an eyebrow. "Like what?"

"You're assuming that torturing her will make her confess. What if you flip the script entirely? Be nice to her instead."

"How is that going to make her want to give back his ring?" Smith asks.

"She was attracted to you the night you met. She wanted you. You can use that to your advantage."

Dan shakes his head. "With the way things are between them now, I doubt she feels anything for him other than wanting to chop his dick off."

I scratch the scruff on my chin, attempting to see things from Shaun's point of view. "What are you suggesting I do?"

"Treat her like you're trying to get in her pants. Send her flowers. Apologize. Tell her you've taken things too far and you'd like to start fresh. Charm the pants off of her. Literally or figuratively."

"Again I ask: How is this going to make her confess to stealing the ring?" Smith asks.

"Once a girl lets you in, once she trusts you, her conscience will eat away at her. Eventually, she'll feel so guilty that she'll have to confess.

Think about it. Is someone going to open up to a jerk who's bullying her every day, or will she open up to someone she has feelings for?"

I cross my arms over my chest. "So you're saying you want me to fake woo her."

"And who knows?" Shaun grins. "Maybe you'll even get laid because of it."

"Or maybe he'll have a sexual harassment case against him," Smith says. "You work with her, Jax. This is risky."

"The man wants his deceased grandmother's ring back," Shaun says. "I say it's worth the risk."

Is it?

CHAPTER TWENTY-ONE

Days Left Until Summer Break: 152
Raegan

"Who's it from?" Sammi whispers.

"I don't know," I whisper back.

"Go check."

"You go check."

"You should see what the card says," Mary whispers.

"What are you crazy bitches doing on the floor?" Kerry's booming voice jolts me and the girls to an upright position.

I clutch my chest. "Jesus. You scared the crap out of us."

"You almost just had more shit on your floor," Mary says.

Kerry looks around my classroom until her eyes land on the object in question. "Who sent you flowers, Rae?"

"That's what we were whispering about," Becca says. "We don't know who sent them to her. Now come in and close the door."

I take a deep breath and approach my desk as if there's a detonated bomb on it. "They're just flowers, right?"

"Maybe they're from Principal Fuckwad and there's a beehive inside."

I freeze mid-step and toss a glare over my shoulder. "Kerr, don't even joke about that."

"You never know. With the shit he's pulled, I'd be careful."

I stretch my arm as far as my body will allow and snatch the card off the bouquet. The girls huddle around me as I pull it out of the envelope.

"Dear Raegan," I read aloud. "Truce? xo Jax."

My jaw drops. I read the card again. And again.

Kerry's the first one to speak. "Is he for real? Why do men always think a bouquet of flowers is going to undo everything they've done wrong?"

I don't respond. I can't. I'm reading the card again.

Mary swipes the flowers off my desk and inspects them, peeking in between the stem of each red rose. "These don't look like a trap. They're just flowers."

Finally, my voice returns. "There's no such thing as *just* flowers. People send flowers for a reason."

"Maybe he realized that everything got way out of hand," Sammi says, ever the optimist. "Maybe he's sorry."

"I don't trust it." Andrea glances at her watch. "You have ten minutes before the bell rings. Go find out what this is about."

Clutching the card in my hand, my heart pounds with every step I take down the hallway. When I enter the main office, Jaxon's door is closed.

"Someone has a secret admirer," Beth says with a smile.

"Did you see who delivered the flowers?"

"Nope. They were here with a post-it that said *Room 1* so I brought them down to your room."

"Thanks. I need to talk to Principal Waters. Is he in yet?"

"He is. Just give a knock."

I walk past her desk and knock on Jaxon's door before letting myself in.

Jaxon smiles when he sees me. "Good Morning, Raegan."

I arch an eyebrow and hold up the card. "What the hell does this mean?"

"Oh, good. You got the flowers. I wasn't sure which ones were your favorite, so I figured I'd go with a classic rose."

"Why?"

He folds his hands on the desk. "I want to call a truce. I did a lot of thinking this weekend, and this whole thing between us has spiraled way out of control. You're an employee and I shouldn't be treating you this way."

"Why now? What changed?"

He hikes a shoulder. "If you say you didn't steal the ring, then you didn't steal the ring. I don't have any reason to believe you did."

I choke on my spit. "Are you kidding me?"

His eyebrows collapse. "What?"

"Just like that? After the past month of hell, you suddenly decide you believe me?"

Jaxon leans back in his chair and runs his fingers through his hair. "I'm sorry, okay? I haven't been thinking straight. My grandmother passed away. Then I got this job. When the ring went missing, I was so angry I blamed the first person I could." He blows a stream of air through his lips. "I'm sorry, Raegan."

I toss the card onto his desk. "You're full of shit. I can see right through your little plan. I'm not as gullible as you think."

He stands and tugs on my wrist as I turn to leave. "Raegan, please. Wait." His hands trail up my arms and cup my shoulders. "The night we met, you read me and my friends in two seconds flat. I know you can tell when someone's bullshitting you. I mean it when I say I'm done with this war we've been having. It's over."

Staring up into his eyes, I don't know what to believe. He seems sincere, but after everything that's happened, I don't want to trust him. I don't know if I can.

Still, he's my boss and I'm tired of the drama at my place of work. If this is what it will take for things to go back to normal, then maybe I have to try.

I sigh. "Did you really think a bouquet of flowers was going to fix this?"

His hands drop to his sides, shoulders slumping forward. "No. I have to start somewhere though."

I cross my arms over my chest. "Tangible items mean nothing to me. Hence me telling you over and over again that I didn't steal the ring."

"Then what matters to you? What do I have to do to gain your trust?"

"Just be nice, Jaxon. Be a good human. Do good for our school. That's all I want from you."

"What about this?" He bends down behind his desk and comes back up with my long-lost shoe in his hand.

Before I can say anything, the bell rings. So I snatch my shoe out of his grip and walk out of his office.

DURING MY LUNCH BREAK, I HIT UP THE STARBUCKS DRIVE-THRU.

I've been thinking about Jaxon's truce all morning. I tried putting myself in his shoes. He invites a stranger into his home, and then his grandmother's ring goes missing. Any logical person would assume the stranger took it. Then said stranger turns out to be his employee ... of course he'd go crazy trying to get the ring back.

Jaxon doesn't know me. The real me. Why should he take my word when I say I didn't steal from him?

Maybe it's time he got to know who I am. No more tricks.

I decide to go along with the truce, knowing there's a 99% chance this is a ploy in his war against me. I'll play along, but I'll remain on guard.

I knock on his open door before heading down to my classroom.

"Hi there."

I approach him like I'm approaching a wild boar. "Hi." I place a steaming coffee and a donut on his desk. "Before you say anything, I swear I didn't put anything in your coffee."

He lifts an eyebrow. "So this is an ulterior motive-free treat?"

"More like an apology treat." I wring my hands as I blurt out what I want to say before I lose my nerve. "I never should've expected you to believe me when I told you I didn't steal the ring. You don't know me. You have no reason to trust me. And with the way I've acted the last month and a half, I don't know why you'd ever trust me. I've behaved totally out of character from the moment I met you. I went through a lot with my divorce, and that's not an excuse but it's the only way I can explain why I behaved the way I did. So, I'm sorry."

His head tilts to the side. "Your ex did a number on you, didn't he?"

I look down at my shoes. "He did, but I think I did more of a number on myself than anything. I just want to leave everything behind me now and start fresh."

Jaxon rises from his chair and walks toward me. I crane my neck to look in his eyes as he advances. His intense gaze commands my attention.

I'm confused by what he's doing until he extends his hand. "Hi. I'm Jaxon. It's nice to meet you."

I bite my lip to keep from laughing as I slip my hand in his. The same goosebumps that shot up my arm the night we met make their reappearance. "Raegan. Nice to meet you too."

"I look forward to working with you this school year."

"Likewise."

He's still shaking my hand when Beth appears at his door. "Knock, knock."

"Look, it's my favorite secretary in the whole world."

Beth rolls her eyes. "Nice try. I'm your only secretary."

I pull my hand out of Jaxon's grasp and tuck a strand of hair behind my ear. "Hey, Beth."

"Hi, my sweets." She surveys my outfit. "You look amazing. Is that hot bod from those kickboxing classes? Because I'll sign up tonight if it'll mean I get to look like you."

I laugh and shake my head. "I also run every day after work."

"Ah, hell. Forget that." She places a paper on Jaxon's desk. "Here's the tutoring information. You should e-mail the staff today to get a head start on things."

"Thanks, Beth. I'll get right on that." Jaxon returns to his chair and powers up his computer.

"Becca and I tutor every year," I say. "Let me know if you need any help with the schedule."

His eyebrows lift. "You want to take point on this?"

"Oh, no. I was just saying I could help you if you have any questions. I wasn't trying to take over."

"It's my job as principal to delegate. I'd rest easy knowing you were the one running the program."

"Really?"

"Really."

"Okay."

"Great." He leans over the desk and hands me the paper Beth had given him. "Here's the information you need to get started. Once you know which teachers are on board, e-mail me their names so I can get them board approved as soon as possible. You'll be getting paid extra for doing the planning, of course."

"Thank you so much. I'll get started right away." I all but skip out of his office and down the kindergarten hallway.

In Becca's classroom, I dangle the paper in front of her face. "Lookie what I got."

She skims it and her shoulders slump. "I don't think I'm going to be able to tutor this year."

"Why the hell not? We've always done it together."

"With William walking and Mia getting potty trained, I can't spend any more time away from home."

"It's only a few hours a week. Can't Jared hold down the fort? It's good money."

She sighs. "Jared isn't willing to do any fort holding of any kind."

"Do you want to talk about it?"

She shakes her head. "Not here."

"Why don't I babysit this weekend? You guys can have a much-needed date night and spend time together without the kids."

Her eyes well. "Is it bad that I don't want to spend time with him?"

I drop onto the chair next to her and put my arm around her shoulders. "Maybe you guys need to talk. You can't go on like this forever."

"I appreciate the offer, Rae."

"Well then why don't you take the kids and come by my place. My mom would love to see the kids. We can have dinner and watch movies in our pajamas."

Becca's face lights up. "I'd love that."

I pull her into a hug before standing. "I'm going to see if Michelle wants to tutor. It's no fun without a buddy."

"That's a good idea. I'm sure she needs the money being a new teacher and all."

I recruit Michelle for tutoring, and make it back to my classroom just in time for the kids to arrive from recess.

Maybe now everything can finally go back to normal.

CHAPTER TWENTY-TWO

Days Left Until Summer Break: 140
Jaxon

*B*eing nice to Raegan is easier than I thought it'd be.

Since I sent her the flowers, she's ceased fire. She still doesn't trust me, but I can't blame her.

I wouldn't trust me either.

With our prank war over, I've been able to focus on the important things, like my job. Tonight's the Halloween dance. Raegan, Michelle, and Chris were the only ones who volunteered to help, so we've been running around all afternoon to ensure everything goes smoothly.

The cafeteria looks incredible. Orange and black streamers hang from the ceiling. Chris brought a strobe light and a smoke machine. Michelle downloaded all the Halloween classics onto her iPod and hooked it up to our sound system.

Raegan hung decorations and crafts her students made. She's currently standing on a ladder hanging a banner. We didn't need it, but she said it would add the final touch. I don't care. I'm holding the ladder steady, pretending not to stare up at her spectacular ass while Chris and Michelle are busy with their backs turned.

"Is it straight?" she asks.

"A little to your left. Too far. More to your right. A couple inches higher. Ah, maybe a little lower. Nope, to your left again."

She whips her head around, a scowl twisting her face as she glares down at me. "Are you fucking with me?"

My lips curve up. "I might be."

She lets out an exasperated sigh and slaps the banner to the wall. "I don't care if it's crooked. I'm getting down."

I chuckle as I extend my hand to help her down, but she swats it away. I'm surprised she even trusted me to hold the ladder for her in the first place. We're making progress.

"Come on, Raegan. I'm joking with you. Just trying to lighten the mood you seem to be in whenever I'm around. You've done a lot for this dance. I appreciate it."

Her eyebrow arches. "Am I missing the insult hidden in there?"

"No insult. Truce, remember?"

She nods and offers me a slight smile. "Sorry. I guess you being nice to me will take some getting used to."

My heart twinges. *Why does that bother me?*

"I'll see you tonight," she says with a wave.

I'd like to tell you I didn't watch her hips sway as she walked away from me, but I can't ... because I did.

I need psychiatric counseling.

"No, Tommy. You can't put your boogers in the juice bowl."

The party is off to a great start.

The cafeteria is packed. Kids are running around and dancing to the music. Trying to wipe their snot on things. You know, fun kid stuff.

Raegan and Chris have been hanging around each other all night. I'd be lying if I said that didn't bother me. The way she throws her head back and laughs—eyes closed, smile wide, truly laughing—twists my stomach. I could be the one making her laugh like that. Instead, she acts like a skittish cat around me. And I hate cats.

Raegan's wearing a black dress with purple and black striped knee-high socks. Her blond hair is hidden under a black wig with a wide-brimmed witch's hat on top.

Chris has on a football jersey. *How original.* Right now, he's gripping her shoulder while he tells an animated story. *Okay, buddy. That's enough.*

I make my way across the room, getting stopped several times by parents with questions about lunch accounts and issues outside in the pick-up loop. Principals are never off the clock.

Once I break free from a group of PTO moms, I stride over to Chris. "Hey, man. Can you do me a favor and watch the snack table? Kids are trying to sneak boogers into the punch bowl."

Chris shudders. "Sure thing, boss."

Raegan's nose scrunches after he walks away. "Is it Tommy Monahan? I already spoke to him twice about that."

"The kid's going to give himself a nosebleed if he keeps digging in his nose like that. Happened to my brother. He was a picker."

Raegan's green eyes peer up me. "You have a brother?"

"I do. He's three years younger than me."

"Huh. I guess even Lucifer had siblings."

I laugh. "Is that one of your names for me?"

She pretends to zip her lips. Then she smiles. "I've always wanted a sibling."

"You're an only child?"

She nods. "My mom had a hard time getting pregnant, so my parents stopped at one."

"You said your mom's a nurse. What does your dad do?"

I wish I hadn't asked because her cheerful expression fades. "He used to be a doctor."

"Used to be?"

"He passed away."

I rest my hand on her shoulder. "I'm sorry."

She smiles but it doesn't reach her eyes. "It's okay."

"It sucks losing someone you love. My grandfather took it pretty hard when my grandmother died. We didn't want to put him in a nursing home, but he can't take care of himself."

"That's such a tough decision. We went through the same with my grandma."

I nod. "I feel guilty because there's only a select few who know sign language. He has to rely on reading lips, which can be hard at times. It will mean so much to him that you've taken the time to learn how to communicate with him."

"It's sweet that you visit him so often. I'd teach my grandmother how to sign if I thought she'd remember the gestures. She seems to have taken a liking to him." She quirks a brow. "You too."

I grin proudly. "Old ladies love me."

"Probably because they're senile."

"What happened to our truce? I gave your shoe back. You're supposed to be nice to me."

She chuckles. "Oh! I love this song. The kids look so adorable doing the dance."

Without thinking, I slide my hand inside hers. "Come on. Let's go show these kids how it's done."

I bite back a smile at the look of shock on Raegan's face as I lead her onto the makeshift dance floor. I swipe the microphone off the stand at the front of the room. "Do you guys know how to do this dance?"

"Yeah!" the students shout.

"All right, Roosevelt Elementary. Let's see your moves!"

I slide my jacket off and hang it on the microphone stand. Hannah, dressed up as Wonder Woman, runs up to me and waves.

"Hey, Hannah! That is the perfect costume for you."

"Thanks. Can I dance with you, Mr. Waters?"

"Of course."

She beams and claims the spot beside me. Once the chorus starts, Hannah and I begin moving to the beat. The other students crowd around us and join in.

Raegan's standing off to the side, watching and laughing as I perfectly execute the steps.

I gesture for her to come dance.

She shakes her head.

I jut out my lower lip.

She crosses her arms.

I lean down and whisper in Hannah's ear. "Go get Ms. Donahue to come dance with us."

My girl Hannah uses her doe eyes and kid pout to coax Raegan onto the dance floor.

Raegan rolls her eyes at me, but she's smirking. "You play dirty, Mr. Waters."

Oh, Ms. Donahue, you have no idea.

THE NEXT DAY, I WALK THROUGH THE DOORS OF THE INDOOR POOL

hoping to see Raegan with her grandmother again. After doing a full sweep of the area, I'm disappointed to find she's not here.

I spend an hour in the water with my grandfather. Halfway through, he asks me why I keep looking at the door. *You're looking for that blond beauty, aren't you?* he signs.

I neither confirm nor deny it, but I don't need to.

Grandpa knows me too well.

He tells me about Annette's dementia. How some days are great, while others are difficult. *If you don't see Annette in the pool for therapy, you can assume it's a tough day,* he signs.

I should've gone home after saying goodbye to Grandpa. I should've headed for the exit and gotten in my car.

But I didn't.

Something's telling me to look for Annette's room. Just to check. Make sure everything's okay.

After one of the nurses directs me to her room, I hop on the elevator and take it to the fourth floor.

I follow the numbers in the hallway until I reach 402. The door is open, but the shades are drawn shut. From where I stand, I can see Annette asleep in her bed.

She's fine, see? Nothing to worry about.

That's when I hear the stifled sobs.

I put one foot in front of the other, entering the room as quietly as I can.

Raegan's in the far corner of the room, curled up in a chair. Her head hangs down, so she doesn't notice me. Her knees are pulled up to her chest, arms hugging them close. Her hair is piled high in a messy bun. She looks so small. So sad. So alone. My heart pulls me toward her until I'm kneeling in front of her chair.

She looks at me from under wet lashes. "Jaxon. What are you doing here?"

"Didn't see you down at the pool. My grandfather said maybe Annette was having a tough day."

Her watery gaze flicks to her grandmother. "She didn't recognize me. She kept asking where my grandfather was. I ... I didn't have the heart to remind her that he passed away a long time ago. She was getting angry so they sedated her."

"Does this happen often?"

"It's getting more and more frequent. I'm afraid I'm going to lose her for good."

I squeeze her arm. "I'm sorry, Raegan."

She blinks. "You came up here to check on her."

I nod, unsure of what her reaction will be. I hope she doesn't ask why, because I don't have an answer.

A lone tear escapes, rolling down the swell of her cheek. I brush it away with my thumb, and Raegan leans into my touch. Without thinking about it, my arms wrap around her. She heaves a sigh and rests her head on my shoulder.

We don't talk. No witty banter. No sarcastic jabs. No flirting.

I might not know why I'm here, but I know one thing for certain: I'll stay here and hold her for as long as she needs me to.

CHAPTER TWENTY-THREE

Days Left Until Summer Break: 139
Raegan

*S*omething has changed.

I can't pinpoint what it is. I can't figure out how it happened. I just know things are different.

Jaxon didn't know that I'd be in my grandmother's room this past weekend. He had no reason to pop in and see if she was okay. He shouldn't have cared.

Yet he did.

Normally I'd be embarrassed to cry in front of a man. Andrew viewed tears as a sign of weakness, and he'd get angry if I cried during a fight. I'd learned to hide my sadness and cry in solitude.

But Jaxon embraced me. Held me as I cried. And I didn't feel ashamed.

I felt comforted.

I flip the light switch in my classroom and set my purse on my desk. A lone yellow rose stands out amongst the stacks of student work I need to grade. Picking it up, I turn over the note that's tied to the stem.

Hope this makes you smile today. Xo Jax

My stomach clenches. A barrage of questions assault my mind, but I push them away as the arrival bell rings. I float around in a daze for the rest of the morning.

When my class leaves for lunch at noon, I sling my lunchbox on my shoulder. I'm halfway to the door when my classroom phone rings.

"Hello, Ms. Donahue's room."

Jaxon's smooth voice filters through the speaker. "Hi."

"Hi."

"Have you been smiling today?"

I bite my lip. "I have. Thank you for the flower."

"Yellow means friendship."

"So we've moved up from a truce to friendship?"

"I'd like to think so."

"I suppose you've earned it."

He chuckles and I imagine what his face looks like with that perfect smile spread across it. "Have a good afternoon."

"You too."

Something has *definitely* changed.

"We're in need of some fundraiser ideas. Parents have grown tired of the same holiday magazines selling candy and candles. Anything you guys can come up with would be greatly appreciated."

Several hands go up around the faculty room. Kerry nudges me. "You should tell him about your idea."

I shake my head. "It gets shot down every year."

"It's a good idea," Becca whispers. "It would be so much fun. The kids would love it."

Kerry raises her hand. "Mr. Waters? Raegan has a fantastic idea that I think you should hear. Ouch!"

I kicked her in her shin under the table.

Jaxon's dark eyes fixate on me. "I'm all ears."

"It's dumb. It'll probably cost more than we raise. No principal before you has ever liked it."

He crosses his arms over his chest. "That sounds like a challenge to me."

A couple of the teachers hoot and clap.

"Come on, Rae," Chris says from the next table. "You always come up with killer ideas."

Jaxon's jaw ticks as he stares at Chris. He recovers quickly and returns his attention back to me.

"Well, we could have a holiday carnival. Games. Music. Cotton candy. A bounce house. Maybe some farm animals for the kids to pet?" I shrug. "The money we make from the tickets can go towards our school. We could do a raffle to get people to donate more money. Teachers or parent volunteers could run the games so we wouldn't have to pay anyone."

"My husband could get us a bounce house," the art teacher says.

"I have an old-fashioned popcorn machine going to waste in my basement," says Mrs. Sullivan.

Mary raises her hand. "My daughter goes horseback riding. They have bunnies, goats, and cows. I can ask how much they'd charge to bring some of the animals over to our school."

Teachers brainstorm ways to make this as cheap as possible for us to put together. Jaxon writes everything down on his pad. All the while, my excitement soars. This idea might actually work.

After the meeting clears out, Jaxon asks me to meet him in his office to go over the details.

"If you have plans, we can do it another time," he says.

"No, I'm free. Let's get started." I turn to Mary before following Jaxon down the hallway. "Call me once you hear back from the farm."

"Will do." She squeezes my shoulder. "This is going to be great, Rae."

I smile. "It will if we can pull this off."

"If anyone can pull it off, it'll be you."

I wave good bye and head to Jaxon's office.

"Let's sit at the table," he says, gesturing to the oval-shaped table.

I take the seat across from him and click open my pen. "I'll make a list of everything we need. You can take a look at the calendar and pick a few dates that will work. Once you solidify a date, you can contact the PTO. We'll also need to make flyers: One asking for parent volunteers, and another for families to purchase tickets. Maybe we should put out a sign-up sheet to form a committee ..." My voice trails off when I notice Jaxon's hand covering his mouth to conceal his smile. "What?"

"I'm sorry," he says. "It's nothing. Continue."

I fold my arms over my chest. "It's not nothing, otherwise you wouldn't be smiling."

"You're so excited about this. It's just ... it's cute."

I laugh. "I just know the kids are going to love this. I get a little enthusiastic sometimes."

"A little?"

"Shut up." I toss my pen at him but he catches it. "I used to be a cheerleader in high school. I have a lot of school spirit. I can't help it."

Jaxon raises an eyebrow. "A cheerleader, huh?"

I roll my eyes and snap my fingers. "Focus, Waters. We've got work to do."

An hour later, Jaxon's tie is off and so are my heels. His shirt's unbuttoned and my hair is in a top knot. I've moved to the floor to give myself more room for my timeline. Things feel comfortable between us. Like we're two friends helping each other out.

My phone buzzes on the table. Jaxon tosses it to me.

"Hey, Mary. What'd they say?"

"They'll bring their animals for free!"

I jump to my feet. "Are you kidding me? Why would they do that?"

"The owner said it'd be great exposure. She said her daughter went to our school, so she'd love to give back."

"That is amazing. I can't believe it."

"I told you this is going to be great."

"Thanks, Mary. You're the best."

"See you tomorrow, Rae."

I end the call and squeal. "We don't have to pay for the animals. That's one less expense to worry about."

Jaxon leans over and crosses it off our list. "That's great news. Looks like we won't have to pay for much. This is amazing, Rae."

I'm beaming when my phone rings again. "It's my mom. She's probably wondering if I'm coming home for dinner."

"We could go grab a bite if you're hungry."

Dinner with Jaxon? I reach for my phone and press the green button while I toy with that idea. "Hey, Mom. What's up?"

"Raegan, are you still at work?"

"Yeah. Why?"

"You need to come home."

"What's wrong? Is everything okay?"

"Uh, I'm not sure. Do you know why the police showed up at my house with a search warrant?"

My face twists in confusion. "A search warrant? For what?"

Jaxon's head whips around, eyes wide as he stares at me.

"Apparently someone thinks you stole a piece of his jewelry, so the police are here to look for it."

My hand clenches around the phone. "I'll be right there. I'm leaving now."

I end the call and my hand drops to my side. *I can't believe I fell for it.*

Jaxon rushes around the table to where I'm standing. "Raegan, I can explain."

My words come out slow and robotic. "You got a warrant to search my mother's house."

"It wasn't my idea. It was my dad. I didn't know he was going to—"

Jaxon's sentence is cut off by the sound of my palm slapping against the side of his face.

My bottom lip trembles and I use all of my strength to fight back the tears. "I knew I shouldn't have trusted you. I knew your truce was a fucking lie!"

"Please, Raegan. Just let me explain."

I shove my feet into my shoes and grab my purse off the table. "I don't have time for your bullshit. I have to get to my mom."

"Let me come with you. I'll tell the police it's a mistake."

"No. Let them search. Let them turn the entire fucking house upside-down. Maybe when they don't find your grandmother's ring, you'll actually believe me when I tell you that I didn't steal it."

I storm toward the door and take off running down the hallway. I'm in my car and at my mom's house in five minutes. Two police cars are double-parked outside. Several neighbors are standing on their porches to watch what's happening.

When I get inside, Mom is on the couch while two police officers rummage through our belongings. I fling myself into her arms, the tears I'd been holding back spilling free.

"Honey, don't cry. Everything's okay. We'll figure this out."

Pulling back to look at her, I say, "I know who sent the police and I know what they're looking for." I glance up at the men. "But they won't find what they're looking for because I didn't steal anything."

"Of course you didn't. That's what I tried explaining to these nice men before you got here. This is a misunderstanding."

"Let's go sit on the porch and I'll tell you everything." Standing, I turn around to face one of the officers. "Please stay and search every square inch of this house. I don't want there to be a shadow of a doubt when you leave."

"Will do, ma'am."

CHAPTER TWENTY-FOUR

Days Left Until Summer Break: 138
Jaxon

"*I* don't understand why you're so mad."

I stop pacing in front of my father's desk. "Because I was finally getting somewhere with Raegan! Now everything is ruined."

"I don't see how it's ruined. If the ring turns up at her house, we'll know it was her."

"And if it doesn't? Then what?"

"Harry said he might be able to get copies of the girl's bank statements to see if there were any big deposits."

"Bank statements? This is getting out of control. I have to work with this woman."

He sighs as if I'm boring him. "You're her boss. You have control of the situation."

I pull my hair through my fingers. "If the ring isn't at her house, this ends here."

"Jaxon—"

"No, Dad! I mean it. I want this to end. Do you hear me?"

He tilts his seat back and crosses his arms, staring at me long and hard.

I spin around and walk toward the door. When I swing it open, Dad calls out to me.

"All of our choices have consequences, son. This is what happens when you take random women home from the bar."

I bite my tongue and slam the door behind me on my way out. I smack into my mother and clutch my chest.

"Mom. Jesus. You scared me."

She points her index finger in my face. "I don't care who it is, but someone in this house needs to tell me what's going on."

"Nothing, Mom. Everything's fine."

Her eyebrows lift. "Oh, everything's fine? You and your brother have been in and out of your father's office, whispering about something you don't want me to know." She plants her hands on her hips. "You are going to tell me, Jaxon."

Giving in, I gesture to the living room. "Let's go sit."

Mom listens as I fill her in on what's been going on since August. She remains quiet, even after I'm finished. I can't tell if she's mad about Grandma's ring, or disappointed in my choices. I definitely wasn't expecting her to say what she says next.

"I'm disappointed in you, Jaxon. I thought I raised you to be a respectful man, and to treat women with kindness."

"What?"

"You're attacking this poor woman with no proof whatsoever. What's wrong with you?"

"All signs point to Raegan taking the ring. I ... I just ..."

"You listened to your father, that's the problem." She shakes her head. "I love that man, Lord knows I do, but he has steered you in the wrong direction. I will deal with him later. As for you, you need to make things right with that girl of yours."

I scrub my hands over my face. "I don't know what else to do, Mom. I don't think flowers and an apology are going to cut it this time."

"You're damn right, they won't. You're going to have to suffer a little while you think about it. This girl sounds like a tough cookie. I like her and I don't even know her."

A smile breaks through my worried features. "She is a tough cookie. She slapped me after finding out about the search warrant."

"Good. You deserve it. I'd have smacked you too."

I laugh. "I know you would've."

"You like her, don't you?"

I shrug and avert my eyes, toying with the frayed edges of the pillow beside me. "I've liked her since the moment I met her. Things just got a little ... messed up after the ring went missing."

"Then you've got to show her you're not going anywhere. You've got to earn her trust back."

"How do I do that when she won't even talk to me?"

"You'll think of a way. It might take some time, but she'll come around."

"How do you know that?"

Mom smiles. "Because she wouldn't be this angry if she didn't like you too."

MONDAY AFTER WORK, I WALK INTO THE NURSING HOME WITH A lead ball in my stomach.

I'm hoping to run into Raegan, though I'm not sure how she'll receive me. She wasn't at the nursing home this weekend. I know she's avoiding me, but I went both Saturday and Sunday anyway.

The police's search proved what I'd suspected: no ring.

Grandpa looks over at me and signs, *Everything okay?*

I don't have the heart to tell him about Grandma's ring. Omitting that part from the story, I try my best to tell him what's bothering me.

I heave a sigh, pushing the pool water around with my hands before signing, *Raegan's mad at me.*

What did you do? he asks.

I laugh. *How do you know I did something wrong?*

He signs while giving me a knowing look. *A woman doesn't get mad for no reason. She gets mad because a man hurt her.*

I nod, swallowing past the lump in my throat. *I did hurt her. But I didn't mean to.*

Grandpa points toward the pool entrance. *So apologize.*

I look up and Raegan's eyes lock with mine as soon as she walks through the door. She stops in her tracks, but Neil says something in her ear to coax her into staying.

I give her space and wait for her to help Annette into the water. She keeps her back turned to me while Neil takes Annette through her exercises.

Go talk to her. Grandpa gives me a nudge.

I swim over to Raegan. She won't look at me, so I swim around her until she can't avoid me.

"Raegan, please talk to me."

Her hands fly to her hips. "I have nothing to say to you."

"You don't have to talk. Just listen. Please let me explain."

She laughs. "Explain what? That the police found nothing in my house? That you're a conniving asshole? That I never should've trusted you? Yeah, thanks. I figured that all out on my own."

"My father had his friend get the search warrant. It wasn't my doing. I didn't know the police were going to show up at your house. I would've told you. I would've warned you."

Raegan rolls her eyes. "Is that all? Is that your explanation?"

My shoulders droop. "I'm sorry, Raegan. Please believe me."

"Believe you? The way you believed me when I told you that I didn't steal your grandmother's ring?" She shakes her head. "Leave me alone, Jaxon."

I do as she asks, and swim back to my grandfather. *She doesn't want to talk to me*, I sign.

He nods and pats me on the shoulder. *She'll come around.*

I don't know that she will. The more I think about this whole thing, the more I believe that Raegan never actually stole the ring in the first place.

But that still leaves me with one question.

Who did?

A WEEK GOES BY AND RAEGAN STILL WON'T TALK TO ME. ASIDE from personal reasons, we need to discuss the upcoming fundraiser. I resort to e-mail.

TO: RDONAHUE@NJ.COM

From: JWaters@nj.com
Subject: Fundraiser

DEAR RAEGAN,

WHAT'S THE HEAD COUNT FOR THE FUNDRAISER? LET'S MAP OUT WHERE *each station will be. I think the animals should go in back of the school, near the playground.*

PLEASE COME TALK TO ME. I'LL BE IN MY OFFICE AFTER SCHOOL TODAY.

SINCERELY,
   Jax

TWENTY MINUTES LATER, A REPLY PINGS ON MY E-MAIL.

TO: JWATERS@NJ.COM
   From: RDonahue@nj.com
   Subject: Re: Fundraiser

DEAR MR. WATERS,

BETH IS COLLECTING THE SLIPS FROM THE ATTENDING FAMILIES. SEE HER *for the head count. I've already drawn up a map. See the attachment.*

NO NEED FOR A MEETING.

·   ·   ·

Sincerely,
  Ms. Donahue

I'M DESPERATE FOR A WAY TO GET HER TO TALK TO ME IN PERSON. I fire a quick e-mail back to her.

To: RDONAHUE@NJ.COM
  From: JWaters@nj.com
  Subject: Re: Fundraiser

DEAR RAEGAN,

THE ATTACHMENT WON'T OPEN. PLEASE PRINT IT OUT AND BRING IT TO my office so we can take a look at it together.

SINCERELY,
  Jax

To: JWATERS@NJ.COM
  From: RDonahue@nj.com
  Subject: Re: Fundraiser

DEAR MR. WATERS,

I FORWARDED THE E-MAIL TO BETH. SHE'S PRINTING IT OUT FOR YOU. Take a look and let me know if there's anything I need to change.

. . .

SINCERELY,
   Ms. Donahue

To: RDONAHUE@NJ.COM
   From: JWaters@nj.com
   Subject: Fundraiser

DEAR RAEGAN,

WHAT'S IT GOING TO TAKE TO GET YOU TO TALK TO ME?

SINCERELY,
   Jax

CHAPTER TWENTY-FIVE

Days Left Until Summer Break: 126
Raegan

The weeks leading up to Thanksgiving break are uneventful.

I steer clear of Jaxon at work as much as I can. We've managed to continue planning the fundraiser via e-mail, and I've resorted to visiting Grandma during the week instead of on the weekend when I know Jaxon will be there.

Maybe he's telling the truth about the search warrant. Maybe I've reacted too harshly. But I can't seem to shake the hurt from my system. Just when I'd let my guard down, he gave me a reason to raise the gates again.

And just like that, we're back at square one.

I'm in Shoprite getting a few last-minute items for Thanksgiving dinner. Every year, Mom and I cook all the holiday classics and bring them to Grandma. We spend the day with her at the nursing home because taking her to our house proved too disorienting for her. She'd get confused and her anger would flare. Everything's calmer where Grandma feels comfortable.

Mom calls for the third time since I arrived. "Yes, Mom. What else did you forget?"

"I don't think I wrote cranberry sauce on the list. Grandma loves the jellied kind."

"Already got two cans in the cart."

"You're the best daughter ever."

"I know, I know."

"See you when you get home."

I end the call and toss my phone back into my purse. As I round the next aisle, my cart crashes into someone else's.

"I'm so sorry. I wasn't—" My words halt on my tongue when I realize who I've crashed into. "Andrew. Hi."

"Hi, Rae." He reaches into his cart and flips open a carton of eggs. "Let's just make sure you haven't ruined my eggs."

My stomach twists, and the apology flies out of my mouth before I can stop it. "I'm sorry. I was on the phone with my mom and I didn't see you."

"Clearly." He deems his eggs satisfactory and returns them to his cart.

"How are you?" I ask, though I don't know why.

"I'm well. Just doing some shopping before the holiday like everyone else."

Oh, me? I'm well, thanks for asking. "Thanksgiving dinner at your mom's as usual?"

A tall, thin red-haired woman struts toward Andrew and wraps her arm around his waist.

"Dinner with Ashley's family this year," he says. "Ashley, this is my ex-wife."

She looks me up and down, and I'm suddenly aware of how frumpy I look. Leggings, fake Uggs, an oversized hoodie, and my hair tied back in a messy ponytail. I didn't get the memo that must've went out about wearing formalwear to Shoprite. Ashley's in a slinky black dress with a fur coat thrown over her shoulders.

Why don't we ever run into our exes when we have our hair and make-up done? It's like one of the laws of physics: An object that looks like trash shall run into everyone she knows while she looks like trash.

"It's nice to meet you," I lie.

"Likewise." Her eyes flick to my boots. "I love your Uggs."

"They're not real Uggs," Andrew says, as if he'd even know the difference. "Raegan only buys knockoffs."

"Oh, how ... thrifty of you." Ashley giggles and rubs herself against Andrew like a cat.

My cheeks are burning from embarrassment when a deep voice startles me from behind. "Baby, did you get the cranberry sauce for Grandma?"

I whip around, mouth agape, to find Jaxon standing tall in a tight, white thermal shirt and dark jeans. The long-sleeve shirt looks like it's painted on, clinging to every bulging muscle. His hair is messy and he's sporting a sexy five o'clock shadow along his jawline.

Maybe I haven't seen him in a while, but *damn he looks good.*

"Who's that?" Ashley whispers to Andrew.

Jaxon flashes his dimpled Colgate smile and extends his hand. "I'm Jaxon."

Andrew shakes his hand, a crease deep between his brows. "You're Rae's new boyfriend?"

Jaxon snakes his arm around my waist. "Well, I wouldn't call me new." He brushes his lips against my temple. "Right, Raegan?"

"Uh, right." *How long has it been now, about four seconds?*

"My baby here was going through a rough divorce when we met," Jaxon says. "The jerkoff she was married to took everything from her. Left her with nothing. What kind of prick does that to a woman?" He shakes his head. "The guy was a real piece of shit."

I bite the inside of my cheek hard enough to keep the smile from splitting my lips. If I get a canker-sore, it'll be worth it just to have seen the look on Andrews face.

And the look on Ashley's face. She rears back from Andrew in disgust. "You told me she made out like a bandit from the divorce."

I laugh. It's the kind of laugh that bursts out of your mouth when you hear something utterly ridiculous. "If you mean leaving me with credit card debt and living at my mom's house, then yeah. I made out like a bandit for sure."

Jaxon feigns surprise. "*This* is Andrew?" He swipes his bottom lip with his thumb as he appraises Andrew, much like Ashley had scrutinized me moments ago. "You're a fucking disgrace."

Andrew squares his shoulders and puffs out his chest. "Excuse me?"

I bump Jaxon with my hip. "He's not worth it. Let his new girlfriend figure it out for herself."

Jaxon turns to me and cradles my face in his large hands, looking into my eyes. "I can't imagine anyone treating you like that. It makes me crazy."

He's really going for it, isn't he?

Just when I think the show's over, Jaxon's head dips down and his soft lips are on mine.

My body stills at first. I'm caught off-guard. My initial reaction is to press my hands against Jaxon's chest and push him off me. But when my hands get there, Jaxon covers mine with his, holding my palms against his racing heart.

And my God *are his pecs made of steel?*

I get swept up in the moment. I forget about Andrew and what's-her-name standing there. I forget that we're in the middle of a grocery store. I forget that I'm kissing the man I'm mad at.

All I can focus on is the way Jaxon's lips feel. Velvety and warm, he takes his time moving them slowly over mine. The kiss is gentle, but I can feel the passion and fervor rolling off him in waves.

He's holding back. *And I don't want him to.*

When his tongue drags across my lips, I open for him without hesitation. Our mouths meld together in synchronicity. I slide my fingers into his hair, gripping on and pulling him closer, deepening the kiss.

This kiss is *more.* More than I remember it being the night I drunkenly kissed him. More than I've fantasized about. More than I've ever been kissed by anyone.

A low groan escapes him when he pulls my lower lip into his mouth and sucks, sending a shiver all the way down to my toes.

Someone passing by mutters, "Get a room," and I snap back to the present moment, in the middle of the cereal aisle.

Andrew and his girlfriend are long gone. I take a step back, lifting my eyes to meet Jaxon's dark, probing gaze. His eyes search mine, waiting for a reaction. Or he's letting realization set in.

I shove him square in the chest. "What the hell, Jax?"

"I saw you turn down this aisle, and I heard the way that asswipe and his girlfriend were talking to you." He shoves his hands into his pockets. "I figured you needed backup."

"And the kiss?"

A smirk tugs at that delicious mouth of his. "I improvised."

I roll my eyes and jerk my cart around him.

"Raegan, wait." Jaxon stops my cart with his foot. "Can we please talk?"

"I don't want to talk to you. I thought I made that clear."

"Rae, I believe you. I believe that you didn't take the ring, and I swear I didn't send those cops to search your house." He pushes his fingers through his hair. "Please. I'm not asking you to forget about everything I've put you through. I'm just asking you to think about giving me another chance."

"Why? Why do you want another chance so badly?"

"Because ... because I ..." He closes his eyes and takes a deep breath. "Because I care. About you, Raegan."

My heart strains against my chest, pulling me toward him. But my brain smacks its hands, like a mother swatting her child away from the cookie jar. "Well, you have a funny way of showing it."

I push my cart down the aisle and leave Jaxon standing there, looking completely deflated.

"I wish I could've seen the look on Andrew's face!"

I fight the urge to smile. "That's not the point, Grandma."

She scoops three more jellied cranberry slices onto her plate. "I don't see what you're so angry about."

"If you kissed him back, you can't hate him that badly," Mom says.

Grandma nods. "There's a fine line between love and hate."

"I liked him before I hated him. That's the problem. It's just … complicated."

"Things weren't this complicated back in my day. Your grandfather took me to dinner and the next day, we were engaged."

Mom laughs. "Not that we want you to do that, Raegan."

"I'm just saying, you don't need to make things so difficult. If Jaxon likes you, and you like him, then you should be together." Grandma leans in toward Mom. "The boy is very good-looking. Their babies would be beautiful."

Mom chokes on her turkey.

I cover my face with my hands. "We're not making babies."

"I don't have much time left," Grandma continues. "I want to meet my great-grandchildren before I die."

"It's Thanksgiving," says Mom. "Can we not talk about your death, please?"

I hate when Grandma talks about not having a lot of time left to live. Part of me, the deep-down part, knows she's right. Guilt twists my stomach when I think about all the time I wasted with Andrew. I could've had children by now. They could've gotten to know their great-grandmother before her mind deteriorates to nothing.

Instead, I'm the only one out of my friends without kids. Without a family of my own. I'm not even *trying* to date or put myself out there. I'm doing what I always do, burying myself in work and preventing myself from finding happiness.

I pull out my phone and send a text in the group chat.

Me: Should I go on a dating site?

Kerry: Yes! *eggplant emoji*

Andrea: Just watch out for dick pics.

Sammi: Yes, you need to start dating.

Becca: Come over this weekend & I can help you make your profile

Mary: I want to come!

Kerry: I'll bring the wine!

Andrea: Take some really good selfies so you can post them. Make sure you can see your boobs.

Mary: But not obvious boobs... more like an inadvertent how-did-those-get-in-there boob shot

Kerry: *coconut emojis*

Me: *face-palm emoji*

I TOSS MY PHONE ONTO THE TABLE. FOR THE REST OF THE DAY, MY mind keeps dragging me back to Jaxon.

That kiss was everything a kiss should be. I shouldn't have wanted it. I shouldn't still want it.

But I did.

And I do.

CHAPTER TWENTY-SIX

Days Left Until Summer Break: 125

Jaxon

That kiss.

That kiss is all I've been able to think about.

I hadn't planned on kissing Raegan. But I saw her standing there, looking so adorable in her hoodie, being put down by her ex-husband and the real-life Cruella de Vil—*who wears fur coats anymore?*—and I just had to do something. It was better than punching Andrew in his ugly dumb face.

I thought for sure Raegan would've slapped me. Again. Or pulled away at the very least. But she kissed me back. That kiss was exhilarating. It lit a fire under me. Within me. All our pent-up feelings for each other are combustible.

And I want more.

I want to burn.

I care about Raegan. I admitted it out loud, to myself and to her. And to whoever was shopping in the cereal aisle. Somewhere along the fucked-up line we've been riding on, my feelings for her changed and grew. We didn't start off on the best foot, but I'm set on changing that now.

Raegan's attracted to me. She doesn't know it yet, but she has feelings for me too. I'm determined to make her realize that.

So Monday morning, I head down to her classroom before the arrival bell rings.

I walk through her open door, and Raegan and her friends are huddled around the computer. I catch a glimpse of a Match.com profile before Raegan minimizes the page.

My gut twists at the thought of Raegan going on a date with some dude off the internet. Any dude, for that matter. But I have to play it cool. I fix my disgruntled expression and smile. "Morning, ladies. I hope everyone had a wonderful Thanksgiving with their families."

"We did, thanks," Becca says.

"How was your Thanksgiving?" Raegan asks.

Her soft hair frames her face, and a cream-colored sweater dress wraps around her curves. *God, she is beautiful.* My eyes flick down to her black knee-high boots and snap back up to her face where it's safe.

I pat my stomach. "It was great. My mom made enough to feed an army."

"That's what moms do best."

I nod. "Well, I don't mean to interrupt but I wanted to check in with you in regard to the fundraiser. Maybe you could meet with me after school?"

"Uh, sure. I have tutoring until four-thirty."

"Come to my office after the students leave." I wave to the girls. "Have a good day, ladies."

I march back to my office like a man on a mission. I'm putting a new plan into place. If Raegan's looking for a match, I'm going to give her one.

I can't let Raegan go on a date.

Not unless it's with me.

IT'S CRAZY HOW ALL YOUR FAVORITE BOOKS AND MOVIES GO RIGHT out the window the second you're asked about them.

Match.com is asking me these ridiculous questions, as if people tell the truth on dating sites. There's no chance Johnny from Brooklyn climbs Mt. Everest in his spare time.

Am I creating a dating profile? Yes.

Am I doing it to go on a date with Raegan? Also yes.

Do I think this plan is actually going to work? Absolutely.

I take the questions seriously and within the hour, I've successfully created my profile. The last step is to upload a picture.

Notice how I didn't say *my* picture. Yeah, this is the part you're not going to like. I'm going to upload my brother's picture instead. We look a lot alike, save for small differences. His nose is bigger. I'm taller. But if Raegan's attracted to me, then there should be no reason why she wouldn't be attracted to Josh.

We'll chat through messages. Then we'll exchange numbers and text. And when it's time to meet on our first date? I'll show up instead of Josh, and Raegan will see how right we are for each other.

Or she'll throw her drink at me and we'll be back to square one.

When I know Raegan's on lunch later in the day, I message her on Match.

. . .

ME: HI RAEGAN. YOU'RE BEAUTIFUL. AND I AGREE: CATS ARE "EVIL demon spawns." Check out my profile and let me know if you'd be interested in getting to know each other a little more. -Josh

SEVERAL MINUTES GO BY BEFORE I GET A RESPONSE. I'M ASSUMING this will be crafted and approved by her friends. *I know how you girls are.*

RAEGAN: HI JOSH. GOOD TO KNOW WE SHARE THE SAME HATRED for those furry creatures from hell. I see you're into swimming. Another thing we have in common. And thank you ... you're quite good-looking too. -Raegan

BOOM. I'M IN. WE CONTINUE MAKING SMALL-TALK UNTIL RAEGAN'S class comes back from recess.

So far, so good.

CHAPTER TWENTY-SEVEN

Raegan

I head down to Jaxon's office after tutoring is over.

This meeting will tell me how things are going to be between us after our kiss at Shoprite. He seemed fine this morning, but the girls were there so I couldn't get a true reading on him.

Someone messaged me on Match this afternoon. I'd be lying if I said the guy didn't remind me of Jaxon. He has the same dark hair and dark eyes. Tan skin. Muscular build. There are subtle differences, but these two could be related.

The whole point of going on Match was to get Jaxon off my mind. Now I find a match with someone who makes me think of Jaxon every time I look at his picture.

Figures.

I knock on Jaxon's door, and he waves me in. I take a seat at the table and set down my notebook and pen. We go over the fundraiser event from beginning to end. Everything has been finalized, and everyone is on board. I'm so excited to see my idea come to fruition. I wonder what we'll be able to buy for the school with all the money we'll raise.

Beth pops her head into Jaxon's office before she leaves. "Mr. Waters, I'm about to head out. I have a parent on hold who would like to speak to you about a bullying situation."

I look up at Jaxon. "I can step out if you want to take the call."

"No. You stay here. I'll take the call at your desk, Beth. Thank you."

"Can I use your computer to type this up?" I ask, waving my notebook. "Then we'll be all set."

"Of course." Jaxon gestures to his computer as he walks out of his office.

I take my notebook to Jaxon's desk and drop down into his chair. "Very comfy, Mr. Waters," I whisper, running my hands along the smooth leather.

I wiggle the mouse to turn off the screen saver. I expect to see Jaxon's desktop. Maybe an open document or e-mail. Instead, a gasp leaves my throat when my eyes register what it is that I'm looking at.

On the screen, clear as day, is Jaxon's Match.com account. But no, it's not *his* account that he's logged into. It's Josh's account.

The Josh who'd been messaging me this afternoon.

My eyes narrow and my jaw clenches. *That sneaky son-of-a-bitch is trying to catfish me!*

I re-read the messages we'd sent back and forth to each other, and I almost laugh. *Almost.*

This guy is a piece of work. He went through all this trouble to create a fake account just to message me. But why? What's his plan? What's the endgame here?

More importantly, what's mine? I've stumbled onto this incredible golden nugget of information. Do I blow up as soon as he walks back into the room? Or do I go along with it and see where this takes me?

I open a Word document and type up the letter for the fundraiser. I pretend all is well when Jaxon strides back into his office.

He smiles at me.

I smile back.

If he thinks he can get *another one* over on me, he is sorely mistaken.

Fool me once, shame on him.
Fool me twice, I am going to end this once and for all.
Here we go again.

CHAPTER TWENTY-EIGHT

Days Left Until Summer Break: 122
Jaxon

*R*aegan and I have been messaging each other for the past few days.

Well, technically I've been messaging her as Josh. But that's a small, tiny, unimportant detail.

She asked to exchange numbers in the last message she sent. It's a good thing. It shows she's into me. But I'm hoping we can stick to texting, and she doesn't want to chat on the phone. There's a chance she could recognize my voice, and this whole thing could blow up in my face.

I realize I'm playing with fire. But there's no way Raegan would agree to go on a date with me. The *real* me. She's still upset about the search warrant and doesn't trust me. Hopefully this plan will help her to see how compatible we are, and how serious I am about wanting to date her.

Or she'll hate me forever and never want to speak to me again.

Really hoping for the former.

My phone dings with a new message including Raegan's number.

My face splits into a wide grin while I save it into my contacts. Then I type out a text and click *Send*.

Me: Hi Raegan, it's Josh.
    Raegan: Who?
    Me: Josh from Match ...
    Raegan: I know I'm kidding
    Me: Funny and pretty. You probably have lots of Joshes lined up for your number
    Raegan: Yet I only gave mine to you
    Me: And why is that?
    Raegan: You're cuter than all the other Joshes
    Raegan: Plus you're the only one who hasn't sent me a dick pic
    Me: Point for me (note to self: delete dick pic)
    Me: Unless you want to see it. This way you know what you're getting yourself into
    Raegan: That sounds like a warning ... does that mean it's really big or really small?
    Me: Guess you'll have to ask me for it to find out
    Raegan: I think I'll pass
    Raegan: But why don't you call me so I can hear your voice instead?

Shit. Now what? I could make an excuse but that would only work for so long. She's right to ask to hear my voice with all the creepy dudes on the internet out there. What are the odds she'll recognize me?

Me: I'm visiting with family at the moment. What about tonight?
    Raegan: Tonight works. How's 8:00?
    Me: It's a date

· · ·

I TUCK MY PHONE UNDER MY CLOTHES AND HEAD INTO THE POOL
with Grandpa.

You look happy, he signs.

I smile and nod.

Raegan's not mad at you anymore I take it?

Things are getting better, I sign. *I'm going to ask her on a date soon.*

Grandpa lifts his eyebrows. *Do you think she'll say yes?*

I think so. I shrug.

Guess I'll find out tonight at eight.

LEADING UP TO THE PHONE CALL WITH RAEGAN, I'M SO NERVOUS I
don't know what to do with myself.

I've folded and put away all my laundry. I hand-washed the dishes
in the sink instead of putting them in the dishwasher. I even Swiffered
the floors. I needed to keep my hands busy.

I twist the cap on a bottle of Jack Daniels and take a swig. I gargle
before swallowing. Then I cough a few times. Maybe if my voice
sounds raspy, Raegan won't realize she's talking to her boss.

You might think this sounds crazy, but I can promise you, it's
nothing compared to how crazy I feel doing this.

At 7:59 I hit the green call button.

Raegan's soft voice sounds in my ear after two rings. "You're a minute early."

I chuckle. "I was excited to talk to you."

There's a pause and I hold my breath, hoping my cover isn't blown.

"Well, you don't sound like a purvy sixty-year-old man, so that's a relief," she says.

"Were you really expecting that?"

"I didn't know what to expect. This is my first time with online dating."

"Same here."

"Were you worried I was going to be a sixty-year-old man too?"

"I was hoping for it. I'll be honest, I'm a little disappointed."

Raegan laughs. The melodic sound sends a shiver through my body. "Good thing you found out now and not on our first date."

"Already thinking about our first date?" I ask.

"Isn't that the whole point of this?"

"It is. I'm glad we're on the same page."

"We seem to be on the same page with a lot of things. It's almost like you read my profile and created yours based on my answers."

I swallow hard. "I could say the same thing about you."

"Touché. So tell me some more about yourself. Your profile says you like to spend time with family."

"Well, I'm very close with my parents. They've been happily married for over thirty years."

"Wow that's great. Any siblings?"

I pause, debating on what to tell her. I decide to go with the truth. "Yes. One brother."

"And are you guys close?"

"We used to be."

"I'm sensing a story there," she says. "What changed?"

"He slept with the girl I was dating."

She gasps. "How long were you two dating?"

"Three years. Two of which she was screwing around behind my back."

Her voice lowers. "I can't imagine what that's like. I'm sorry."

I shrug. "Everything happens for a reason, right?"

"That's what they say."

"Do you believe it?"

"I don't know what I believe. It'd be nice to think that everything happens the way it's supposed to. That you're led to the people you're meant to be with. Maybe we are, and some people are only supposed to be life lessons instead of permanent fixtures." She laughs softly. "I really sound divorced, don't I?"

"Nothing wrong with that. How long were you married?"

"Seven years."

"Why did it end?"

"He wasn't who I thought he was."

"Who did you think he was?"

"Someone I could count on. Someone who'd treat me the way I always dreamed I'd be treated by the man who loved me."

"The guy's a dick."

She giggles. "You don't even know him."

Yes, I do, and it only took two seconds to come to that conclusion. "He had you and he didn't treat you right. It's simple. The guy's a dick."

"I won't fight you on that. If it's any consolation, your ex is a bitch."

I tilt my head back and laugh. "We're a sorry pair."

"Speak for yourself."

"What about your family?"

"My parents were happily married too."

"Were?"

"My dad passed away a few years ago. Now it's just me and my mom."

"I'm sorry. How did he pass, if you don't mind me asking?"

"Heart attack. He was working outside in our backyard. He'd mowed the lawn and picked weeds. Then he came inside and just collapsed." The line goes silent for a few seconds. "He went quickly and didn't suffer. But we didn't have time to say goodbye."

My chest tightens. I remember how sad she looked the day I found her crying in her grandmother's room, and imagine her burying her father at such a young age. I want to wrap my arms around her and hold her again.

"You still there?" she asks.

"I'm here. I'm so sorry you had to go through that."

"All right, enough of this doom and gloom. Let's talk about something less grim."

"Ready for my dick pic now?"

She laughs. "Tell me about your job."

I'm about to tell her how much I love being a principal when I catch myself. "I'm, uh … an accountant."

"Do you enjoy it?"

I think back to the times I've heard Josh talk about his job. "I like working with numbers. Helping people save and invest their money. It's not as meaningful as your job though. That must be fun."

"It can be. It's a tough job but I love what I do. I love working with kids." She pauses. "We got a new principal at my school this year so that's been interesting."

My stomach drops. "Man or woman?"

"Man. It's the first time we've had a male principal since I've been at my school."

"Do you like him?"

"He's good with the kids. They love him."

"And you?"

She sighs. "I don't know. He's a little arrogant."

"Arrogant?" I choke out, trying to regain my composure. "How so?"

"He has this way of ordering people around. He forced me into being the school's mascot during an assembly once, and he signed me up for a voluntary dodgeball event. He's kind of a bully."

I stifle a laugh. "That's rough. The guy sounds like he's on a power trip."

"You have no idea."

Oh, I do. "About that first date … how does next Friday night sound?"

"I mean, I'll try to fit you into my schedule."

"You can cancel with all the other Joshes. I'll be the only one you need."

"You're confident. Careful now. You're starting to sound like my boss."

I sit up straight and clear my throat. "Uh, how does dinner at seven sound?"

"Sounds good to me. Just text me the address of wherever we're going and I'll meet you there."

"Will do. I'm excited to meet you, Raegan."

"Me too. Glad you're not a sixty-year-old man."

I chuckle. "Same here."

She yawns. "I'm going to call it a night."

"Okay. I'll talk to you tomorrow."

"Goodnight, Josh."

I let out a breath and toss my phone onto the coffee table. That went better than expected.

Let's hope our date next week goes just as well.

CHAPTER TWENTY-NINE

Days Left Until Summer Break: 119
Raegan

I haven't seen much of Jaxon the week leading up to our date.

I use the term *date* loosely. It's more like we're approaching the final round in Mortal Kombat. I'm about to finish his ass.

I *have* been talking with "Josh" every chance I get. In fact, he calls me every night before I go to bed. We talk for hours, and I find myself forgetting who's really on the other side of the phone. Our conversations are effortless. We laugh and flirt. When we hang up, I'm left with a false sense of hope. Why can't Jaxon really be Josh? Or do I want Josh to really be Jaxon?

Whatever. You get my point. This is confusing.

But if Jaxon's plan is to fuck with my head, then I'm going to need to fuck with his twice as bad. Tonight, I'm kicking my texting up a notch.

ME: HEY. WHATCHA DOING?

Jaxon: Cooking dinner. Thinking about you.

Me: You cook?

Jaxon: *picture*

Me: That looks delicious. I love shrimp.

Me: Take a selfie. Let me see you cooking.

Jaxon: *picture*

Me: Did you take your shirt off just for that picture? Or are you really cooking with no clothes on?

Jaxon: No point in wearing clothes when I'm here alone.

Me: Don't burn yourself. Hot oil splatters.

Jaxon: Let me get this straight. I send you a picture of my dinner and you tell me how delicious it looks. I send you a picture of my sexy body and all you can think about is cooking safety?

Me: LOL good point. Let me try again …

Me: Daaaaaammmmmmmnnnnnn you look fine

Jaxon: I feel like you're being sarcastic but I'm going to pretend that you're not

Me: Totally not being sarcastic. I've looked at your abs 5 times since you sent it.

Jaxon: Really?

Jaxon: I mean, of course you did. *sunglasses emoji*

Me: I guess it's only fair that I send you a picture back

Jaxon: YES. YES YOU SHOULD.

Me: *picture*

Jaxon: I'm not even sure what I'm looking at. Is that your ankle?

Me: Sexy, right?

Jaxon: Hottest ankle I've ever seen

IF I'M GOING TO MESS WITH JAXON, I NEED TO COMMIT TO THIS 100%. I stand in the middle of my bedroom and strip down to my bra and thong. He's already seen me in a bathing suit, right?

After inspecting myself from every angle in the mirror, I take a deep breath and proceed with the next phase in my plan.

· · ·

ME: I'M JUST KIDDING. THIS IS WHAT I REALLY MEANT TO SEND.
    Me: *picture*

TWO SECONDS AFTER MY HALF-NAKED SELFIE IS DELIVERED, MY phone rings.

"Hello?"

"I can't believe you just sent me that picture."

I giggle. "You sent me a half-naked picture, so I figured I should return the favor."

"I'm not complaining. I just didn't expect that."

"Good. Now tell me what you thought of it before I start to get self-conscious."

"I think your body is perfect, Raegan. You're sexy as hell."

I bite my bottom lip and close my eyes, digging deep for any extra courage that's being stored inside me. "I wish you were here right now."

He pauses. "Where are you?"

"In my bed."

I hear movement, like he's shuffling around.

"Josh, you there?"

"I'm here."

"What are you doing?"

"Just put my food to the side and came to my bedroom."

My plan is working. "What about dinner?"

"My food can wait. All I can think about right now is you in your bed."

"Are you looking at my picture?"

"I am."

"Tell me what you'd do if you were here."

Another long pause. He needs to know I'm serious. I have to give him a little nudge.

"Josh, do you want me to start?"

"Yes," he rasps. "You start."

"I'm touching myself right now," I lie. "I'm looking at your picture and pretending it's your fingers that are sliding under my panties."

He groans. "How do you feel?"

"Wet. Warm. I want you to touch yourself too, Josh."

"Already there, babe." His voice is low and desperate sounding. I imagine how he looks, pumping himself in his hand, looking at my picture.

"Good. Now tell me what you'd do if you were here."

"I'd peel those panties off and I'd taste you. I'd rub my tongue over your wet pussy, back and forth. Your hands would be in my hair, pulling me closer, holding me where you want me. Your legs wrapped around my neck, my tongue gliding over you nice and slow."

I swallow, sweat beading along my skin. I'm wondering if this is what he did when he went down on me the night he took me home, cursing myself for being too drunk to remember it. I'm so wrapped up in what he said, so turned on by the thought of his tongue on me. What started as a game has turned into incredibly hot phone sex, and I don't want to stop. I might've been in control at the start of this, but Jaxon has taken the reigns now.

My shaky hand trails down my body. *Here goes nothing.* "Then what?" I whisper.

"Then I'd dip my fingers inside you while I swirl my tongue over your clit."

I push my fingers inside myself and circle my clit with my thumb, pretending it's Jaxon who's taking care of me. I let out a moan as my hips roll into my touch.

"You'd beg for me to let you come, and when you do, you'd scream my name over and over again." He exhales. "God, Raegan, I want to do that to you so badly."

"I want that too."

He groans again, and I nearly come undone at the sound. I have to stop Jaxon's name from escaping my lips, yet it doesn't feel right to use the fake name he gave me. I don't want Josh. I don't want anyone else.

I want Jaxon.

I want Jaxon kissing me. I want Jaxon touching me. I want Jaxon to make love to my body.

My heart and mind race, each one pulling me in opposite directions.

His deep voice cuts into my thoughts. "I want you to come for me, Raegan. I want to hear you."

This isn't part of the game. It's wrong. It makes no sense. But right now, I don't care. Without another thought, I let go. I fall over the edge, and Jaxon comes with me. We're moaning and panting, diving into ecstasy together.

When it's over, we're quiet. I guess this is the phone sex version of cuddling.

Realization sets in for the both of us. He's pretending to be someone else, and I'm pretending I don't know who he really is.

"Raegan?"

"Yeah?"

"That was ... that was ... wow."

I smile. "I know."

"I can't wait to see you Friday."

Me too, Jaxon. Me too.

CHAPTER THIRTY

Jaxon

*H*oly *fuck*, that just happened.

CHAPTER THIRTY-ONE

Days Left Until Summer Break: 117
Raegan

"You do realize you're not actually going on a date, right?" Becca asks.

I chose to get ready at her place so she could help with my hair and make-up. "I want to look good when I burst Jaxon's bubble. I'm catfishing a catfisher. Maybe I should've called Nev. I could be famous."

"I still can't understand why he'd create a fake Match account. You're obviously going to find out it's him when you go on this date. It doesn't make sense."

"I can't understand *anything* that man does."

"Are you going to hear him out first? Are you going to tell him you knew it was him this whole time? I wish I could be a fly on the wall."

"Want me to bring Mia's walkie talkies?"

Becca's eyes widen. "Really?"

"No." I swipe my bottom lip with clear gloss and press my lips together. "Done. How do I look?"

"He's going to die when he sees you in that dress. You look amazing, Rae."

I treated myself to a new outfit for tonight: a tight, black, long-sleeve dress that stops just above mid-thigh, paired with black ankle boots. The dress is low-cut, but there's a sheer overlay covering my chest. Cleavage with class. It was a little on the expensive side, but totally worth every penny. I need Jaxon to feel the magnitude of his mistake when he watches me walk away in this dress.

Maybe I'll finally get my slow-motion walking scene!

I don't have a plan going into this. I need to see how it unfolds. Hear what Jaxon has to say for himself before I make my move. My stomach twists in anticipation.

Jaxon avoided me at work. He can't bring himself to look me in the eye after our phone sex. I bet the guilt of pretending to be someone else is eating him alive.

"You look nervous," Becca says. "Maybe you should get there early and have a drink before the showdown."

In a poker match, the final round is referred to as the *showdown*. It's when two players reveal their cards to see who's holding the stronger hand.

The analogy is fitting, because tonight, I'm going all in.

I TEXT "JOSH" TO LET HIM KNOW I'VE ARRIVED. THEN I ORDER A shot of whiskey and down it.

I'm sitting at the bar, waiting. I have the perfect view of the front door from the reflection in the mirror behind the bar. At five-to-seven, Jaxon waltzes in.

My stomach clenches. He's in an olive-green V-neck sweater. The color compliments his skin tone, making him look all the more tall, dark, and handsome. His hair is messier than it usually is at work, more like it was when he kissed me at Shoprite.

Don't think about that kiss. Not now.

It's showtime.

I watch as he talks to the hostess. She gestures toward the bar, and his eyes sweep over to me. He hesitates before taking the first step, wiping his hands on his slacks and squaring his shoulders. He's nervous.

Good. He should be.

Jaxon takes the stool to my left and clears his throat. "Hi, Raegan."

I turn my head and do my best to look surprised. "Jaxon? What are you doing here?"

He fiddles with his watch, eyes bouncing around the room. "I, uh ... I'm here on a date."

I smile. "That's nice. Where is she?"

His dark eyes lock with mine. "Right here, actually."

My eyebrows pinch together. "What do you mean?"

He opens his mouth but the bartender stops in front of him and asks, "What can I get you?"

"Just a water, please."

We wait in silence while the bartender fills Jaxon's glass. He slides it over, and Jaxon gulps it down.

"Jaxon, what's going on?" I ask.

"I know you're here on a date," he says. "You're expecting a man named Josh."

"How do you know that?"

"Because I ... I'm Josh."

I sit back against the stool and cross my arms, making him wait for my reaction. "Explain."

He exhales through his lips. "I saw that you were on Match. I knew you'd never agree to go on a date with me, so I made an account under someone else's name. I figured if you got to know me, you'd feel the connection between us and then maybe you would agree to give me a chance."

What? He wants to date me? I hold his gaze but say nothing. This isn't what I expected. My mind goes blank and I can't think of anything I'd planned on saying to him.

"Raegan." He reaches out and takes my hands in his. "I know everything is screwed up between us, and I know I'm to blame for that. I know you don't trust me, but I want to prove myself to you. I want to show you who I truly am. I want *you*."

I look down at the way he's holding my hands. At the sincere, pleading look in his eyes. *Is this really why he created Josh's profile?* I was prepared for a prank. I was prepared for the usual conniving Jaxon. But this?

The heat rises inside me, and I feel the words coming to the surface. I pull my hands back. "I knew it was you all along."

Jaxon's hopeful expression falls. "What?"

"I saw fake Josh's profile on your screen when I used your computer last week. I knew you were trying to trick me, so I decided to go along with it. The messages, the phone calls. I knew it was you the whole time. So your big plan to trick me? It's not going to work."

Jaxon puts his hands up. "Wait, Raegan. You've got it all wrong. This wasn't a plan to mess with your head. I didn't lie about anything we talked about. Everything I told you was the truth."

I choke out a laugh. "Everything except for your identity. Kind of a big omission, don't you think?"

"I know, but I only said I was someone else because I didn't think you'd go out with me if I'd asked you."

"You're right. I wouldn't have. And this is why! You lie and scheme to try to get your way. It's all you've done since I met you. So tell me:

What was the real point of all this?" I look up at the ceiling. "Is there a bucket of pig's blood waiting to drop onto my head? What were you trying to gain?"

"Nothing! This isn't some prank. I know it wasn't the best idea, but I didn't know how else to go about it. I just wanted another chance with you. A clean slate." He scrubs his hand over his jaw. "I would never try to hurt you, Raegan. I care about you."

My head is spinning. I don't know what to believe. I have to get out of here. I slide off the stool and sling my purse onto my shoulder. I step into Jaxon's space, my index finger jutting into his chest. "I'm not a toy you can play with whenever you feel bored. I'm tired of the games, and I'm sick of the lies."

"Says the girl who pretended she didn't know it was me. Why did you go along with it? Why not confront me as soon as you found out?"

"Don't turn this around on me! This is about you."

"I think you wanted it to be me. I think you liked knowing it was me on the other side of the phone." Jaxon leans forward, that damn sexy smirk curving his lips. "Especially the other night."

I scoff. "Don't be ridiculous. I was just fucking with you."

His lips are at my ear, and he whispers, "Didn't sound that way."

My skin prickles. I can't think straight when he's this close to me. I place my hand on his chest and push him out of my space.

Jaxon catches my hand and holds it there against his chest. His heart races beneath my touch. "No more games, Raegan. No more lies. No more pranks." His eyes bounce between mine. "I'm laying it all out on the table."

How easy it would be to melt into those muscular arms right now. His scent is intoxicating, his gaze hypnotizing. Every nerve ending in my body is tingling, screaming for me to give in and kiss him.

But intoxication dulls your sense, and hypnosis controls you. That's not what I want for myself. I can't give in. I need to stand my ground. Be strong.

Protect myself.

"I don't want you. Stay away from me, Jaxon." I yank my hand back and turn towards the exit.

I storm out of the restaurant and through the parking lot. I don't stop moving until I'm in my car. My hand is on the shifter, car in reverse. I stare into the rear-view mirror, waiting to see if Jaxon will come after me. One second ticks by, two, three ...

Half a minute later, my shoulders drop and I pull out of my parking spot.

CHAPTER THIRTY-TWO

Days Left Until Summer Break: 113
Jaxon

"*T*he bounce house goes right there on the grass. The animals can go around back."

The fundraiser starts in thirty minutes, and everything is going according to plan. No hiccups. No issues. It's smooth sailing.

Raegan did an incredible job. Tonight's event will raise a ton of money for our school, and it's all because of her.

We haven't spoken a word to each other since the night of our date that wasn't. I'd hoped she would come around once she took some time to think about everything I'd said. I'd hoped she cared about me the way I'd grown to care about her. But she didn't. And she doesn't.

"I don't want you."

The pain is all too familiar. Me wanting a woman who doesn't want me back. So I ignore the twinge in my chest and push her out of my brain. I've got a school to run, and that's what I focus on.

Once the fundraiser starts, students and their families surround the building. Music blasts through the speakers. The scent of popcorn and cotton candy fill the air. It's a brisk night, but nobody seems to mind. Everyone's too busy having fun.

I walk the perimeter of the school, thanking parents and high-fiving kids.

I spot Raegan by the animal pen, and decide to congratulate her on her success.

A goat nuzzles her hand as she strokes his head. He's smaller than the other goats, and he keeps climbing onto the rungs of the fence to get closer to Raegan.

"Looks like you made a friend," I say, sidling alongside her.

Raegan doesn't take her eyes off the goat. "His name is Jeffrey."

I reach my fingers into the pen and scratch behind Jeffrey's ears. "Nice to meet you, Jeffrey."

Jeffrey backs away and rams his head into the gate.

Raegan giggles. "He keeps doing that. The owner, Carol, said he's the craziest goat she's ever had. He doesn't like to be with the other goats, and he's always trying to escape."

Jeffrey runs into the gate again.

I chuckle as I kneel down. He sticks his nose through the fence and licks my hand. "Poor guy doesn't like to be locked up. Can't say I blame him."

Raegan's quiet. I look up at her and say, "You did a great job with this fundraiser."

She shrugs, looking out across the field. "Hopefully it raises a lot of money."

"It will." I stand and wipe my hands, brushing off the grass from my pants. "Thank you for doing all this. The school's lucky to have you."

"Jaxon—"

Raegan's words are cut off as Jeffrey leaps over the fence and takes off running across the grass.

"Shit," I mutter. The owner is busy giving pony rides, so I bolt after the goat. Really wishing I'd worn something other than my suit and dress shoes.

Jeffrey zigzags in front of me. Every time I reach out to grab him, he darts in the opposite direction.

"Jeffrey!" Raegan calls from a few feet behind me. "Come back!"

He bleats and keeps running. *This little fucker is fast.*

"You go left, and I'll go right." Raegan forks off and attempts to catch him, diving onto the grass. She slides through the mud and almost grips his hind leg, but Jeffrey runs right past her.

Jeffrey heads toward the school. The doors are propped open so families can use the bathrooms. It might cause a bit of a scene but if he runs into the building, I'll be able to corner him.

Raegan and I successfully herd him inside. The goat loses traction on the tile, slipping all over the hallway. This slows him down. I catch up to him in seconds, and dive toward him when I get close enough.

"Gotcha!" I grip his hind legs and pull him into my arms.

Raegan skids to a stop behind us. "Oh, thank God." She hunches over, hands on her knees, gasping for air.

Jeffrey bleats as I sit up and cradle him. "Sorry, bud."

A smile tugs at Raegan's lips. Then a giggle escapes her, and next she's full-on belly laughing.

I grin. "What's so funny?"

"We just ... chased a goat ... around the school." She can barely get the words out, tears springing from her eyes.

Jeffrey bleats again and I laugh along with Raegan. "Pretty sure he just told you to go fuck yourself."

She smacks her leg as she doubles over, laughing even harder.

Carol, the owner of the runaway goat, appears in the doorway. "Jeffrey!" She slaps her palm against her forehead. "I am so sorry about this, Mr. Waters. The goat is nuts!"

I hoist myself up as she takes Jeffrey from me. "It's okay. He just wants to run free."

Carol shakes her head. "I've gotta get a taller fence." She scurries back into the hallway, scolding Jeffrey along the way.

I lift my jacket to my nose and grimace. "Great. I smell like a farm animal now."

Raegan giggles, wiping her eyes. "I can't remember the last time I laughed that hard."

"You should do it more often. It looks good on you."

"Never a dull moment with you."

"I'm going to take that as a compliment."

"You would."

I want to continue our usual banter, but Raegan's words replay in my head: *Stay away from me, Jaxon.*

My smile falls. "Well, enjoy the rest of your night. I won't take up any more of your time."

She looks like she wants to say something, but I don't give her the chance. I head for my office, leaving her alone in the darkened classroom.

It's just after eight-thirty and the fundraiser is over.

The teachers and I clean up the schoolyard while the families clear out of the parking lot. I wish the staff Happy Holidays and tell them to enjoy their week-long break. Then I head back into the building.

I'm at my desk when Raegan shows up in the doorway of my office. She's covered in mud and grass stains from the Jeffrey fiasco, her cheeks splotched with red from the cold December air. "Are you staying here all winter break?"

"Just wanted to finalize a few things so I don't have to think about them next week."

"Doing anything fun?"

I shake my head. "Just spending time with family and friends, relaxing."

"Same here."

"You deserve a break from all your hard work. Have a nice week off." I turn back to my computer and continue typing.

She steps into my office and sits in the chair opposing my desk. "Could we ... can we talk?"

I arch an eyebrow, keeping my gaze fixed on the screen. "I thought you wanted me to stay away from you."

She huffs out a sigh. "I think we should talk."

"Do you, now? Because I've wanted to talk for a while, yet you refused to give me the time of day." I can't stop the hostility in my tone.

"You can't blame me for being mad about everything you've done, Jaxon."

"And what about everything *you've* done? You're not innocent in this, Raegan. You've been a willing participant this whole time."

Her eyebrows skyrocket. "A willing participant? As if I had a choice when you forced me to be the mascot, or play in the dodgeball game? You caused this shitstorm between us, Jaxon. But your arrogant head is so far up your ass that you can't see it."

"Deflect all you want. You stooped just as low as I did, and you know it."

The red in her cheeks deepens. She rips her jacket off and tosses it onto the chair as she stands. "You called a truce. Then you went and fucked it up all over again by having my house searched for that godforsaken ring!"

Good, I've struck a nerve. I rise from my chair and stalk around the desk. "If you would've let me explain, you'd know that I had nothing to do with that search warrant. But that's your problem, Rae. You get mad and run away, instead of facing the problem and talking it out."

She steps toward me and jabs my chest with her finger. "It's impossible to talk to you. I feel like a yo-yo being jerked around. One second you're nice Jaxon, and the next you're coming at me with another scheme!"

I catch her hand and grip it in mine, pulling her closer. "There was no scheme. But you won't listen to anything other than the cowardly voice in your head."

"Cowardly? This coming from the man who hid behind a fake Match profile."

"I did that because you wouldn't talk to me. You wouldn't give me a chance to explain myself."

She rolls her eyes. "And lying about who you are is a great way to get me to open up."

I drop her hand and tug on the ends of my hair, looking up at the ceiling. "God, you're so infuriating."

"The feeling is very mutual."

"We could go 'round and 'round this circle, arguing about everything that has transpired up until this point. But if we want to move forward, we have to be honest."

"I have been honest," Raegan spits. "You're the liar."

"Fine. Then admit you enjoyed talking to me on the phone for the past two weeks."

"You mean while I was talking to the fake person you created?"

I step into her space, edging her backward until her ass hits my desk. "You knew it was me. You knew you were talking to me, and you liked it."

She crosses her arms and narrows her eyes. "I was just trying to get back at you."

"No, you wanted me to see you in your bra and panties that night. You touched yourself thinking about me. Not fake Josh. *Me.*" I push my fingers through her hair and cradle the back of her head, running my nose along her neck. She shivers as I make my way up to her ear. "So if we're being honest right now, I'm gonna need to hear you say it."

"I was faking it," she whispers.

I take her earlobe between my teeth, biting gently on her soft skin. She stifles a moan, still trying to deny the truth.

"Didn't sound like you were faking it." My hands slide down her body, cupping her ass and pulling her against me. "I know you want me. I know you want me to touch you, lick you, make you feel good."

Her eyes squeeze shut as she grips my shirt in her hands. But she doesn't push me away.

"I need to hear you say it, Rae." My lips graze over hers as I whisper, "Tell me you want me."

She opens her eyes and spears me with them. Seconds tick by before she speaks, a silent debate passing between us.

"I want you, Jaxon."

Those four words are the shot at the starting line, and I crush my mouth against hers. Our tongues waste no time finding each other, plunging in, winding around, all with the force of a speeding roller coaster. The kiss is deep. Furious. Passionate. My hands leave Raegan's ass and come up to tangle in her hair, holding her mouth in place so she knows I have no plans on stopping.

Her fingers work the buttons on my shirt, but they're small and she's impatient. She rips the damn thing open, buttons scattering around my office, and it's my undoing. Any semblance of control is lost. I tear her sweater over her head and yank her jeans down, tossing each annoying garment aside before rushing right back to reclaim her mouth. I kick out of my slacks and we're finally skin to skin.

I lift Raegan onto my desk, sweeping everything that's in my way off the surface. Papers and pens fly around us like confetti. Her legs are spread, locked around my waist, and she's panting against my mouth. I pop open the clasp on her bra and take her beautiful full breasts into my hands.

"God, I've wanted this for so long." My voice sounds strangled, gruff with the desperation of a madman. I kiss down her neck, grinning at the sound vibrating from her throat. When I suck her nipple into my mouth, Raegan digs her fingernails into my shoulders and arches her back.

I don't stay there as long as I'd like to. Perfect tits like hers deserve to be worshiped. But I'm not taking things slow. There'll be time for that later. Right now, I'm on a mission. I begin my descent, kissing a trail down her stomach. I push her lace thong to the side and cover her wet, throbbing lips with my tongue. *This.* This is what I've been waiting for.

I sink down to my knees and pull Raegan toward me until her ass is hanging off the desk. Her legs over my shoulders, her grip on the back of my head, holding on while her hips rock against my mouth. I dip two fingers inside her, working them in sync with my tongue as I lap up her sweetness.

Within seconds, Raegan breaks apart. She screams my name and her body shudders as I feel her clenching around my fingers. Watching her come is the best damn thing I've ever seen. I've never been more turned on in my life.

With a beautiful flush across her skin, Raegan drops her feet to the floor and stands. Her palms slide down my chest, down my stomach, and her fingers hook onto the waistband of my boxer-briefs. She peels them off and my dick springs free, bobbing, hard and ready for her. Her eyes take me in, and then she looks up at me from under heavy lids and says, "Sit."

I collapse into my chair, watching as Raegan straddles me. *Fucking Christ.* My eyes are on hers, those forest green eyes that mesmerized me the first night we met. I suck in a breath as she grinds against me, gliding back and forth, covering me with her wetness. I reach up and pull her mouth to mine, kissing her with so much want and need.

"You're so fucking beautiful, Raegan."

"Jaxon," she whispers, breathless.

I know what she wants. I want it too. I pull open the drawer behind her and fish for my wallet, our lips fused together. I must fumble for too long because Raegan looks over her shoulder and takes the condom from my wallet. She tears it open and rolls it over my length with hungry eyes.

She lifts up and then sinks down on me, slowly, savoring the feel of every inch as she takes me inside her. We both groan, and my head falls back while she molds around my dick. She pulls me almost completely out before sliding all the way back down. Raegan rides me, slow and controlled. It's a blissful kind of torture.

Nothing has ever felt this good.

The way she's twisting her hips, the way she feels, warm and tight, taking me deep ... I'm not going to last. I wrap my arms around her and thrust, harder, faster, slamming her hips down onto me again and again.

"Yes ... Jaxon ... yes."

I circle my thumb over her clit and Raegan goes over the edge again. She throws her head back and comes, hard, her entire body contracting on top of me. I'll never get tired of hearing her scream my name like this.

With her still in my lap, I stand up and spin her around. She must know exactly what I want because she leans over and slaps her palms onto the desk in front of her.

"That's my girl," I whisper in her ear. "Spread those pretty thighs for me."

I'm officially ruined. I'll never be able to rid myself of the sight of Raegan bending over my desk with her legs wide open.

I push myself inside her and reach down to touch her legs, her hips, her breasts. Every inch of skin I can get my hands on while I plunge into her over and over. And just when I think this can't get any hotter, Raegan brings my hand to her lips and takes my middle finger into her mouth. Her tongue wraps around my finger as she sucks on it, and pulls it out slow with a pop. Then she places my hand between her thighs.

Holy fucking shit. This woman is going to kill me. Maybe that's her plan. Now ask me if I care. I'd gladly die right here, just like this.

I play with her clit until she comes. Again. That's three times, in case you've lost count. I pick up the pace, driving inside her harder and faster, our bodies slapping against each other. Raegan arches her back, pushing her ass against me, meeting me thrust for thrust.

The buildup over the past few months finally releases as the scorching-hot pleasure shoots through me. I let go. I curse and call Raegan's name, coming harder than I've ever come in my life. I collapse against her back, reveling in this moment, both of us breathless and utterly spent.

I pull out of her and get rid of the condom. I sit back in my chair and pull Raegan down with me, wrapping my arms around her and kissing her swollen lips.

"Jaxon, that was ..." She rests her forehead against mine. "That was incredible."

I run my fingers through her hair and look into her eyes. "Does this mean you're not mad at me anymore?"

Raegan giggles. "Yeah. I'm pretty sure that's what this means."

CHAPTER THIRTY-THREE

Days Left Until Summer Break: 90
Raegan

"*H*appy New Year. How was your break?"

My heart skips a beat when I recall my week with Jaxon. "It was great."

Beth wags her finger at me. "I know that look, Rae. Tell me everything! Who is he?"

I giggle and cover my burning cheeks with my hands. "Is it that obvious?"

"You just floated in this office on a cloud. Now spill."

"I met a guy on Match."

Beth flings her arms around me. "That's great news. I'm so happy you're putting yourself out there."

"It's still very new, so I'm not telling too many people."

Beth zips her lips. "My lips are sealed."

I spent most of my winter break holed up in Jaxon's apartment. It was strange going back there, but Jaxon said we were starting over with a clean slate. We made new memories in that apartment. Delicious, sex-filled memories.

Before I left, I asked him if he wanted to strip search me to make sure I didn't steal anything. He didn't think it was funny at first, but then I actually let him strip search me so everything was fine after that.

I haven't told anyone what's going on between me and Jaxon. Not the girls. Not Becca. Not even my mom. The less people that know, the better. It's frowned upon for a principal to date a teacher in the same school. Neither of us wants to be moved, so we agreed to keep things under wraps for now. At least until the end of the school year.

It's crazy to think that we're dating after everything that happened between us. But I'm not complaining. I wanted him before I hated him, and even then, a part of me still wanted him.

I gesture to Jaxon's closed door. "Is Mr. Waters in yet?"

Beth's smile falls. "I'm afraid he won't be in for a few days."

"What? Why?"

"His grandfather passed away. He called me late last night."

My stomach twists. *Why didn't he call me?* "Oh. That's sad."

Beth nods. "Poor guy. Spread the word. Maybe we can collect a few dollars from everyone today and send him a fruit basket or something."

I swallow past the lump in my throat and make my way to the door. "That's a great idea, Beth. I'll let everyone know."

I head down to my classroom and close the door. Pulling my phone out of my purse, I see there's a new text from Jaxon.

JAXON: GOOD MORNING, BEAUTIFUL. CALL ME WHEN YOU GET this.

I CLICK ON HIS NAME AND HE ANSWERS ON THE FIRST RING. "HEY."

"Beth just told me about your grandfather. Jaxon, I'm so sorry. You should've called me."

"I didn't want to wake you." He sounds tired. "Figured I'd catch you before you got to work and saw that I wasn't there."

"What happened?"

"The doctor at the nursing home said he had a stroke. They tried to revive him but ... I guess his body was too weak."

My heart strains in my chest. "I wish I could be with you right now."

"Me too, babe."

"When's the wake?"

"My mom's on the phone with the funeral home now."

"Text me when you have the information."

"I will."

The bell rings and I frown. "I'll call you when I get out of work."

"Okay. Have a good day, gorgeous."

I sigh. "I'm really sad about your grandfather."

"So am I. He would've been happy to know that we're together. He liked you."

I smile as tears prick my eyes. The morning bell cuts into our conversation and I groan. "Gotta go. I'll call you after work."

I walk into the funeral home alone.

Jaxon didn't want everyone from school showing up to pay their respects, so he told Beth it was a private service.

"You don't have to come," he'd told me earlier. "I know you want to keep things between us a secret, and I understand."

But I couldn't bear the thought of not being beside him to hold his hand through this. So I swallowed my nerves and showed up.

I linger at the back of the room, spotting Jaxon with his family by the casket. Samuel looks at peace. At least he's with his wife now.

I wait for the crowd to clear before making my way toward Jaxon. Relief floods his face as soon as he sees me, and he wraps me in his arms.

"I'm so glad you're here," he whispers.

"I wouldn't let you go through this alone."

He sighs against my hair, holding me to his chest.

I pull back to look at him. Dark circles underline his bloodshot eyes. Lifting my hand, I caress his cheek. "I took the day off tomorrow so I can come with you to the funeral."

He leans into my touch and closes his eyes. "I'm the luckiest man alive."

"And who might this be?" We both turn to face the woman standing beside us. Tall and slender with dark hair, she smiles warmly. It's the same smile that Jaxon has.

Jaxon wraps his arm around my waist. "Mom, this is Raegan."

I extend my hand. "I'm so sorry for your loss, Mrs. Waters."

She waves my hand away and pulls me into a hug. "It's so nice to meet you, Raegan. I've heard so much about you."

I lift an eyebrow at Jaxon before his mother releases me. "All good things, I hope."

She laughs softly. "Thank you for coming. I hope you'll come back to the house for dinner later."

"Oh, I don't want to intrude on your family time."

"Nonsense," she says. "As Jaxon's girlfriend, you're part of our family now. Oh, there's Mrs. Filmore. Excuse me."

Jaxon pinches the bridge of his nose. "I'm sorry about that."

I smile and squeeze his arm. "She's sweet."

"You don't have to come back to the house if you don't feel comfortable."

"Do you want me to come?"

"Of course I do."

"Then I'll be there."

My eyes skate over to where Jaxon's father is standing several feet away. I know it's him because Jaxon's the spitting image of him. Tall and tan. Dark, intimidating eyes.

Eyes that are zeroed in on me.

That's when I remember: Jaxon's father had been the one to get the search warrant. Jaxon believes that I didn't steal his grandmother's ring ... but his father might not share that same belief.

"So, Raegan, how long have you been teaching at Roosevelt?"

"Six years."

"Aren't there rules about dating a staff member?" Jaxon's brother, Josh, asks.

The real *Josh.*

I look around the table, hoping my face isn't as red as the tomato sauce in my bowl. "Well, we plan on keeping things quiet until the summer. We'll figure out what to do from there."

"Ah, yes. You're a professional when it comes to keeping things quiet."

Jaxon's hand balls into a fist. "Don't fucking start, Josh."

"Make sure you check her purse before she leaves."

Jaxon pushes out of his chair, but I pull his arm.

Mrs. Waters puts her hand up. "Enough. I don't want to hear another word about that ring. Raegan is a guest in this house and you will treat her with respect."

Josh mutters something inaudible before chugging the remainder of his scotch, his third glass.

"I know it must be hard to believe," I say. "I'm a stranger and the ring is gone. But I can assure you that I didn't steal anything from your family, and I'd never do anything to hurt Jaxon."

Jaxon squeezes my knee under the table, and the conversation ends there.

We continue eating in silence. Jaxon's father hasn't said two words to me since we were introduced at the funeral home. I hate that my presence is causing such a strain on the family, especially during such a sensitive time. But if Jaxon was able to trust me, then I have to hope that his family will too.

After the awkward dinner, I help Mrs. Waters clear away the dishes. She's been so kind and understanding. *At least* she's *on my side.*

I excuse myself to the bathroom. When I emerge, Josh is standing in the hallway looking at the pictures hanging on the wall. His eyes are glassy and he's swaying like he's on a boat.

"Jax and I used to be best buds," he says. "Now he hates me."

"Sleeping with your brother's ex will do that to you." I shouldn't have said that, but I couldn't help myself.

"He gets everything. The golden child."

"He *earns* everything by being a good person."

Josh laughs. "He's in love with you, you know. Do you love him?"

I roll my eyes. He's slurring his words and trying to stir up trouble. "Excuse me." I try to push past him, but he grips my bicep.

"I saw the way you look at him. You love him."

"I don't see how that's any of your business."

Josh digs into his pocket and pulls out a blue velvet box.

A ring box.

My eyes widen and it feels as if all the air has been sucked out of the hallway.

"I'm going to put this in your purse," Josh says. "If you love Jaxon, you'll put it back in his apartment and you won't say a word about it."

I yank my arm away. "Why the hell would I do that?"

"This family is already hurting over the loss of my grandfather. Do you really want to make things worse and tell Jaxon that I was the one who stole it from him?"

"You have got to be kidding me." Both our heads jerk to the left. Mr. Waters is standing at the end of the hallway.

"Dad, I ... it wasn't me," Josh sputters, backing away from me.

"I just heard everything you said." He seizes the ring box and flips it open, looking down at the sparkly ring inside. His jaw works under his skin. "Get away from Raegan, and get in your room. I can't even look at you right now."

Josh hangs his head and disappears down the hall.

I press my hand against my chest and let out the breath I'd been holding. "I'm so glad you heard what he said."

"I'm sorry he put you through that." Mr. Waters steps toward me and slips the ring box into my purse.

My body stills. "What are you—"

"Josh is right. I can't have my family fighting anymore. You need to get this back to Jaxon without him knowing."

My jaw drops. "With all due respect, sir, I don't want any part of this. Jaxon searched his entire apartment. Don't you think he'll find it odd if the ring suddenly appears?"

He crosses his arms across his chest. "He'll think he misplaced it. Then this will all be over. This is your chance to make things right."

Tears well, threatening to spill out onto my cheeks. "Mr. Waters, I ... I don't think I can—"

"Everything okay in here?" Jaxon walks into the hallway, eyes volleying between me and his father.

Mr. Waters smiles. "I was just showing Raegan some of our pictures."

Jaxon puts his hand on my shoulder. "You okay? You look like you've seen a ghost. My hair wasn't that bad back then, was it?"

"I actually don't feel very well. Would you mind if I went home?"

"Of course not. Do you need me to drive you?"

"No. No, I'm okay to drive." I place my hand over my stomach. "I have a stomachache."

It's not a total lie. My stomach is twisted in knots.

All because I'm now carrying a detonated bomb in my purse.

CHAPTER THIRTY-FOUR

Days Left Until Summer Break: 84
Jaxon

I haven't seen Raegan since she left my parents' house.

She caught the stomach bug that's ripping through our school. She took a few days off and was sick throughout the weekend. I keep asking her to let me come over and take care of her, but she insists that I'll catch it. Plus she hasn't told her mom about us yet.

So I've resorted to phone dates instead.

"Have you thought about what you want to do for Valentine's Day?"

"I think we should stay at your place," she says. "I don't want to chance anyone seeing us if we go out to a restaurant."

"I really hate that we have to hide this from everyone."

She sighs. "I know."

"We don't have to go anywhere. I can cook."

"You don't have to make a big deal about it. It's just a silly holiday."

"It's not silly to me. I want to spend it with you."

"Who knew you were such a softie?"

I chuckle. "You sound like you're feeling better."

"I'll be back at work tomorrow."

"That's great. I've missed you."

"I've missed you too, Jaxon."

We say goodnight and I lie awake thinking about Raegan.

She's perfect in every way. I'd been drawn to her when she walked into that bar over the summer, and now I know why. She's stunningly beautiful. Smart as a whip. Heart of gold. Our sex, our banter, everything we share is more than I could've asked for.

The night she showed up to my grandfather's wake, it hit me.

I'm falling in love with her.

And on Valentine's Day, I'm going to tell her.

CHAPTER THIRTY-FIVE

Days Left Until Summer Break: 80

Raegan

*a*s if I couldn't feel any more guilty for lying to Jaxon about his grandmother's ring, he has to go and be the world's best boyfriend.

I glare at the two-dozen red and pink roses sitting on my desk. "Can you put them in your room? I can hear them mocking me."

Becca pats the top of my head. "At least you got flowers. I doubt Jared even knows what day it is."

I groan and slump over onto the desk. "Stupid Valentine's Day."

"More like stupid Josh. And stupid Jaxon's father." She shakes her fist in the air. "I can't believe they're putting you up to this."

I caved and told Becca everything. I'm surprised I held out for this long. Girls physically cannot keep a secret from their besties. It's a gene that's missing from our DNA. Besides, I know she won't tell anyone, and I really needed some logical advice. I was going crazy racking my brain for solutions to my problem.

"I'll have to move to a new state and change my name to Isa Montgomery." *That's a little drastic,* Becca had said. *Plus you'll miss me too much.*

"What if I leave the ring on Jaxon's doorstep, knock on his door, and flee the scene?" *You'd trip over your own two feet and Jaxon would see you on the ground when he opens the door.*

"I could just tell Jaxon the truth." *Then you'd be dating someone whose family hates you. Or they'd deny your story and Jaxon would think you've had it this whole time.*

"So what the hell am I supposed to do?" *Hide the ring in his drawer and be done with it.*

Becca's always the voice of reason. So tonight, I'm going to Jaxon's apartment and I'm ending this ring bullshit once and for all.

WHEN I WALK INTO JAXON'S APARTMENT, THE SCENT OF SAUTÉED garlic and onions fill my nostrils.

"Damn, it smells good in here."

Jaxon closes the door behind me and takes my coat. "I'm making tacos."

My eyes widen. "You really are the perfect boyfriend."

He chuckles and dips his lips down to meet mine. "God, I've been dying to kiss you for days."

I stretch up onto my toes and wrap my arms around his neck. "Prove it."

"What about the tacos?"

"This is the only scenario in which tacos come second."

Jaxon lifts me up and I wrap my legs around his waist as he carries me to his bedroom. I'm still clutching my purse like a life preserver. My plan is to plant the ring in his drawer when he goes to the bathroom.

If only I could get rid of it *before* we have sex. It's difficult to focus on anything over the taunting tick-tock coming from my purse. *Now I know why Captain Hook was so afraid of that sound ...*

Jaxon drops me onto his bed. I watch as he undresses, my eyes taking in every inch of his perfect, chiseled body. But it isn't his shredded abs, his blocky shoulders, or his muscular arms that make my heart thunder in my chest. It's the feeling I get when I look into his eyes.

I'm falling in love with Jaxon.

"What?" he asks.

I scoot to the edge of the mattress and kneel, running my fingertips along his smooth chest. "I love ... when you take your clothes off."

Chicken shit.

Jaxon smirks. "I love when I'm not the only one who has his clothes off."

I lift my sweater over my head, and begin tossing my clothes onto the floor. I pull him down with me as I lay back on the bed.

"You're right," he says against my lips. "This is much better than tacos."

I smile and reach for a condom in his nightstand. After I roll it over his length, I prop myself up on my side. "Can we do it like this? I want to be close to you."

Jaxon turns onto his side, facing me, and hooks my leg over his. "Baby, we can do it any way you want to."

We both sigh as he pushes inside me. We're intertwined like two ropes, arms and legs twisted around each other's bodies. My hands in his hair, pressing his face close to mine. His hands on my ass, guiding my hips as he thrusts into me. We don't speak as much as we normally do. This time feels different. It feels like more. The sound of our breaths and moans of pleasure fill the quiet as we gaze into each other's eyes.

I love this man.

I do. Somehow, through all of our fighting, through the anger, the diarrhea, and the dodgeball, I fell in love with the enemy.

That notion sends me over the edge. "Yes, Jaxon. Oh, God. Yes!"

As I float back down to earth, Jaxon caresses my face, looking at me in a way that melts my insides. Emotion swirls in those deep, dark irises of his.

Does he feel the same way I do?

It's my turn to ask, "What?"

"I love you, Raegan. I love you so much."

My heart hammers in my chest. I run my fingers through his hair, swallowing back the sentiment. "I love you too."

Jaxon kisses me, slow and passionate, and he finds his release. Then he's holding me against his chest wearing the biggest smile. I've never seen him so happy.

My stomach twists. Josh was right. How can I hurt the man I love? It would wreck him to know his brother stole the ring, and that his father wanted to help him keep the secret. As much as I hate carrying this lie with me, I'd hate to be the one to cause Jaxon that kind of pain.

Jaxon hears the churning of my stomach and laughs, assuming I'm hungry. "I'll get our tacos."

My eyes follow him as he rolls out of bed and disappears into the hallway.

Now's my chance.

I want to be rid of this ring, this burden. I jump out of bed and remove the ring from my purse, eyes darting around the room. Putting it on top of the dresser where he'd had it before would be too obvious. I need to hide it in a place where he'll find it—just not while I'm here.

Blood pulses in my ears while I pull out the top drawer as quietly as I can. With a shaky hand, I tuck the ring box underneath a few T-shirts.

Will he find this here? I shake my head and try shoving it in the corner of the drawer instead. I need to make it look like the box fell inside on accident. Maybe I should set it on the dresser and slide it into the open drawer so it looks legit ...

"What are you doing?"

I jump at least an inch off the floor. Jaxon's standing in the doorway, with a plate of food in each hand. He's staring at the blue box I'm clutching, blinking as if he's unsure of what he's looking at.

I'm naked, hunched over his dresser, holding the ring in my hand. *This isn't a good look for me.*

"Jax, I can explain."

The plates clatter onto the top of the dresser. Lunging toward me, he snatches the box out of my hand and flips it open. He shakes his head, disbelief written all over his face. "What the hell is this, Rae?"

"It's ... it's your grandmother's ring."

"I know it's her ring," he fires. "Why do you have it?"

I hadn't prepared myself for this. What should I do? Tell him the truth, and shatter his world? Or tell him a lie, and shatter his world? Either way, Jaxon's going to be hurt.

But family is everything. I don't want Jaxon to lose that because of me.

"Raegan, why do you have this?" he asks again.

I take a deep breath, and decide to do the right thing.

Even if it feels wrong.

"I didn't want you to find out like this. I thought I could slip it into your dresser without you knowing it was me."

"No. It can't be you." His eyes well as he shakes his head. "Tell me it wasn't you."

My bottom lip trembles. I don't need to say anything else. My silence says it all. All I can do now is watch as Jaxon's heart breaks.

CHAPTER THIRTY-SIX

Jaxon

"*G*et out."

I thought I'd been hurt before. I thought I knew what deception felt like. My ex cheated on me with my brother. They'd lied to me about it for a long time.

Yet in comparison, this feels much, much worse.

I think I'm in shock. I'm not yelling at Raegan as she collects her clothes. I should be livid. I should be telling her what a conniving liar she is. Instead, I'm rooted to the floor, clutching the ring box, staring at the open drawer.

I stand there for a while. Long after Raegan walks into the hallway and slips out the front door.

How could she lie to me? I'd been so sure that Raegan didn't steal the ring.

Why tonight? Why now, of all times, did she decide to give the ring back?

What else did she lie about? She told me she loved me. Was that a lie too? Was this all part of her plan?

I rub my forehead, the questions assaulting my brain. I don't have any of the answers, and maybe I never will, but one thought sticks out among the rest: I don't want this ring.

I throw my clothes back on and take the ring with me on my way out.

"JAXON, WHAT ARE YOU DOING HERE?"

I drop a quick kiss to my mother's cheek as I enter the house. "I need to talk to Dad."

"He's in his office. We just finished dinner. Are you hungry?"

"No," I say over my shoulder as I stalk down the hallway. When I reach the office, I swing the door open without knocking.

"Jaxon." My father looks at me over his glasses. "What are you doing here?"

I toss the ring box onto the desk in front of him. "I don't want this."

His eyebrows pinch together as he stares down at the box. "You found Nana's ring."

"You can give it to Josh if you want. Or keep it. I don't give a fuck what you do with it. Just keep it away from me."

"Jaxon, what's going on?" Mom's in the doorway behind me.

I stare at the floor when I say, "Raegan had the ring."

"What do you mean she had it?" Dad asks.

I sigh, raking a hand through my hair. "She came over tonight. I found her trying to hide it in my dresser."

Mom shakes her head. "That can't be right."

"Of course she had it," Dad says. "I knew she had it all along."

His comment stokes my anger. "You were right, Dad. You were right and I was wrong. Does that make you feel better?"

"Calm down, son. I know you're upset but—"

"You don't know anything!" I storm out of his office and crash into Josh in the hallway.

"I knew that little bitch had Nana's ring," he says, a smug look on his face.

I press my forearm against Josh's neck and slam him against the wall. "Call her a bitch again," I say through gritted teeth.

"Jaxon!" Mom pulls on my shoulder. "Jaxon, enough. Let him go."

Why am I sticking up for Raegan? I'm losing my mind. I have to get out of here. I push off of Josh and head for the front door.

"Please don't leave like this," Mom calls after me.

"I'm sorry, Mom. I have to go."

I need to be alone right now.

CHAPTER THIRTY-SEVEN

Days Left Until Summer Break: 73
Raegan

"*A*unt Raegan, wake up!"

I groan and shield my eyes from the sunlight streaming through my window. "Leave me alone, you little Gremlin."

Mia giggles. "It's lunchtime. Mommy says you have to get up and eat something."

"Tell Mommy I'm not hungry."

"Mommy!" Mia screams. "Aunt Rae said she's not hungry!"

I cringe and flip the covers over my head, cocooning myself in the warmth. *I shall stay here forever.* I'll become one with my bed. They'll make a show about me. *True Life: I'm Living in My Comforter.*

"Raegan, you need to get up."

"Your mommy tone won't work on me, Beck."

She sighs. "Mia, get off the bed, please."

Mia bounces onto her bottom and springs off the bed. "What are you gonna do, Mommy?"

It's quiet. Quiet is never good.

"Becca?" I call from under the blanket.

The next thing I know, my mattress tilts upward and I'm rolling sideways onto the floor.

"Why didn't I think of that?" my mom asks.

Mia squeals. "My turn! I want a ride!"

I rub my backside and glare at the traitors before me. "I hate you all."

Mia crawls onto my lap, uninvited. "Aunt Rae, you need to brush your hair."

"She needs a weedwhacker at this point," Becca says to my mom.

I hold Mia's chubby little face in my hands. "I'll buy you a puppy if you get your mother out of my room."

In a flash, she's up and pushing on Becca's legs. "Mommy, hurry! You need to get out so I can get a puppy!"

"Mia, your aunt is lying. You can't trust a word she says right now. She's not herself."

Mom scoops Mia into her arms as she pouts. "Come on. You can help me make lunch. We can cut our sandwiches into hearts."

"Yay!"

I shake my head. "If only our problems could be solved by cutting our sandwiches into hearts."

"Raegan, you can't hide in here forever. Take a shower and come downstairs for lunch. You'll feel better once you're clean and fed."

"What am I, a dog?" I stand and slide my mattress back onto the frame. "Nothing's going to make this better."

Becca sighs while I flop onto the bed and burrow under my covers. I hear the click of the door closing and release a breath. *Finally, alone again.*

Several minutes later, the doorbell rings. Then I hear voices in the hall.

My bedroom door bursts open, Kerry's voice booming. "All right, ladies. Mary, Sammi, you two take her legs. Becca and Andrea, you're gonna have to help me get her arms."

"Be careful," Mary says. "She's scrappy."

Before I can make a run for it, my friends seize my limbs. I'm helpless as they lift me off the bed and carry me out into the hall.

"Get off me! Are you crazy?" I squirm, trying to free myself from their grasps.

"Watch her head," Andrea shouts.

"This might actually be easier if we knock her unconscious," Kerry whispers.

The girls wrangle me into the bathroom and toss me into the tub. They hold me down while Becca twists the knobs to the faucet. Ice cold water rains down on me.

"It's freezing!" I scream. "Get me out of here."

"You'll come out when you don't smell like a barnyard animal." Kerry squeezes shampoo into her palm and begins scrubbing my head.

"You're getting soap in my eyes, you asshole!"

"This ain't a picnic for us either."

I don't know if it's the suds stinging my eyes, or if I'm finally giving up the fight, but hot tears spill over my lids. My head hangs down as the sobs rip through me.

Becca climbs into the tub beside me and wraps her arms around my shoulders. One by one, my friends huddle around me, getting soaked by the spray of the shower head.

"It's going to be okay," Sammi says.

I cover my face with my hands. "I didn't think it would hurt this bad, taking the fall for something I didn't do."

Andrea squeezes my knee. "You were trying to do the right thing by Jaxon and his family."

Mia appears in the doorway. Her mouth drops open when she sees all six of us crammed on top of each other, fully clothed, in the tub.

I open my arms for her and she crawls onto my lap, ducking under the stream of the water. "Are you sad, Aunt Rae?"

"I am."

"Do you want to ride in my Barbie car? That always helps me when I feel sad."

I giggle. "Maybe later you can take me for a spin."

"Come on," Becca says, standing. "Let's let Aunt Raegan finish her shower."

"Towels are in the hall closet."

The girls exit the bathroom, leaving a trail of water on the tile floor. I pull the shower curtain closed and strip out of my wet pajamas. I let a few more tears escape, pressing my forehead against the wall.

Why does doing the right thing have to hurt so bad?

CHAPTER THIRTY-EIGHT

Jaxon

*A*nother day without Raegan.

She's called out sick every day this week. I wonder why. She wasn't the one who was lied to for six months straight. I should be the one vegging out at home, drowning my sorrows in a bottle of Jack Daniels.

But I've got a school to run. So I do what I do best and bury myself in work.

It's Friday and the school's buzzing. We're supposed to get hit with a snowstorm this weekend, which means there's a chance we could get Monday off.

"Wear your pajamas inside-out this weekend," Beth calls as she swings her coat on.

"Will do." *Not.* I don't want a snow day. If it were up to me, I'd come to work all weekend just to avoid the deafening silence in my apartment.

The school clears out. Teachers speed out of the parking lot, busses depart with excited students.

It's almost four o'clock when I hear whispers outside my office.

"Who's there?"

The whispers stop.

"I know you're out there. I can hear you."

Becca peeks into my office. "Hi, uh, Mr. Waters."

"Becca. What's going on?"

"Do you have a sec?"

"That depends. What is this in reference to?"

Becca closes the door behind her and sits in the chair facing my desk. "I think you need to know the truth."

My skin prickles. "About?"

"About your grandmother's ring."

I shake my head and wave my hands. "No. I'm not discussing this with you."

She leans forward. "You don't have to say anything. I just need you to hear me out, and then I'll be gone."

I pinch the bridge of my nose and close my eyes. "You have thirty seconds."

"Thirty seconds? Geeze. Not really a lot of time. Let's see. Where do I start ..."

"Twenty seconds."

"Okay, okay." She sits up straight and pins me with her gaze. "Your brother is the one who stole the ring."

"Time's up. Get out of my office."

"I still have, like, ten seconds!"

"Fine. Hurry up." I cross my arms and rock back in my chair.

"The night Raegan came to your house for dinner, after your grandfather's wake, your brother cornered her in the hallway. I think he was drunk, but that doesn't matter. He told Raegan that if she loved you, she would plant the ring back in your apartment and never tell you about it. But your dad caught them. He heard everything Josh said. He agreed with Josh, and forced the ring into Raegan's purse."

Becca blinks, waiting for my reaction.

Josh? My father? Heat rises in my neck, and it's suddenly hard to breathe. "Look, Becca. I don't know what kind of crazy lie Raegan concocted but she's the one who stole the ring. It's pretty sad that she's trying to use my family against me."

Becca's shoulders droop. "I know this is difficult to digest, but it's the truth. I was the one who told Raegan to go along with your brother's idea. I thought it'd be the best way to get your ring back to you without any drama. But now she's heartbroken and I feel like it's my fault."

"You're her best friend. Why would I believe anything you're telling me right now?"

"Because if Raegan was lying, I wouldn't be in here corroborating her story." She stands and smooths her blouse. "I know you have no reason to trust me, and I get it. But you fell in love with her for a reason. Trust your gut. Listen to your heart. It won't steer you wrong."

I sit in my office for a long time after Becca excuses herself, lost in thought.

I wouldn't put it past Josh to steal the ring. He'd be a likely suspect in this case. But my father? Why would he protect Josh? Why would he lie to me? And why would Raegan go along with it?

Any way I slice it, someone's lying to me.

But I need the truth. I need answers.

It's time I go get some.

"Jaxon, what a pleasant surprise."

I pull my mother into my arms and hug her tight. "I'm sorry I've been ignoring your calls."

She touches her hand to my cheek. "I understand."

"Are Dad and Josh home? I think it's time we had a talk."

"They're here. I'll go get them. Would you like something to drink?"

"I'll take a glass of Dad's scotch."

Mom eyes me warily. "Maybe a cup of coffee? It's not even five o'clock, Jax."

"It's five o'clock somewhere." Josh waltzes into the living room wearing a smirk. "At least that's my motto."

I slide my jacket off and hang it on the coat rack. "Have a seat, Josh. I'm here to talk to you and Dad about something."

His lips twitch. He falls onto the couch cushion and places his hands behind his head, propping his feet on the coffee table.

"Mom hates it when you do that," I say.

"Always a momma's boy."

My jaw clenches. I take a seat on the loveseat on the other side of the coffee table. Dad enters the living room with Mom in tow.

"Jaxon, is everything okay?" He sits beside Josh, while Mom takes the spot next to me. *A faceoff, how fitting.*

My leg bounces as I draw in a breath. "I know the truth."

Josh sits up ramrod straight.

Dad remains calm. "The truth about what?"

"I know Josh was the one who stole Nana's ring from my apartment."

Mom gasps. I didn't expect her to be in on this, and I'm glad I have her on my side.

My brother is silent, a rare occurrence for him.

"I'm afraid I don't know what you're talking about," Dad says.

"No? Do you know anything about cornering Raegan in the hallway the night of Grandpa's wake?"

"Honey, what is he talking about?" Mom asks.

Dad shakes his head. "The girl is trying to mess with your head. She's a liar. That's what she does."

"Raegan didn't tell me anything."

"Then how do you know?" Josh asks.

My eyebrows shoot up. "So you admit it then?"

"I ... uh ... I didn't say that."

"Josh, shut your damn mouth," Dad hisses.

My jaw goes slack and I sit back against the couch. The image of Raegan's face that night in the hallway pops into my head. Her eyes were wide as she stood beside my father. She'd said she wasn't feeling well. She'd refused to see me for days after that, blaming it on a stomach virus. If Dad forced her to take the ring, that would explain everything.

Becca was telling the truth.

Mom's voice rises. "Joshua Stephen Waters, I need you to start talking, and you'd better tell the truth. What did you do?"

Josh scrubs his hand over his face. "I took the ring, okay? I used Mom and Dad's spare key and I let myself into your apartment while you were out celebrating your promotion."

A volcano erupts in the pit of my stomach. My hands start to shake. "Why the fuck would you do that?"

"Because I wanted you to know what it feels like to screw up! For once in your life, I wanted you to be the one Dad was disappointed in."

"The only reason Dad's disappointed in you is because you do shit like this!" I rise off the couch and lunge toward Josh, gripping the collar of his shirt in my hands. "You are fucking pathetic."

"Jaxon! Please, stop this," Mom cries.

Dad separates us, shoving me backward. "Enough."

"And you," I snarl, facing my father. "You're always cleaning up Josh's mess. Maybe you should let him fall on his ass so he'll learn his lesson."

"I'm sorry, Jaxon. I saw an opportunity to end the ring fiasco without anybody getting hurt, and I took it."

"Well your plan backfired. I saw Raegan with that ring and do you know what she did? She took the fall. You're the one who betrayed me, yet she accepted the blame for it. So I hope you're fucking happy, Dad. I'll never step foot in this house again."

I storm to the door, yanking my coat off the hook.

"Jaxon, wait." Mom tugs my elbow, a tear rolling down her cheek.

"I can't stay here with them for one more second."

"I know. I understand how betrayed you feel."

She knows because she feels the same way. I lift my hand and wipe Mom's tears. "I'm sorry about all of this."

She shakes her head and grips onto my shoulders. "You have nothing to be sorry about. Go talk to Raegan. She'll understand and everything will be okay."

I swallow the boulder in my throat and nod.

I really hope she's right.

CHAPTER THIRTY-NINE

Raegan

"The snow's really coming down."

I pull the blanket closer to my chin. *Good.* I'm looking for any excuse to remain a hermit in my house for another few days before going back to school. Before I have to face Jaxon.

Let's go, Mother Nature. Show me what you got.

"Have you decided on a movie?" Mom asks.

I stare at the television. I've scoured the guide for the past half-hour, making sure to skip quickly over any romantic-looking movies. It's now between *Texas Chainsaw Massacre* and *Chucky*. I hate scary movies, but I'd rather have the shit scared out of me than cry into my bowl of popcorn while Cameron Diaz gets the guy in the end.

"Let's watch *Texas Chainsaw Massacre*. That Chucky doll creeps me out."

Mom stifles a groan. "Isn't there anything else you'd like to watch?"

"It's blood and terror, or I'm going back to my room."

"Fine." Mom flops down onto the couch beside me and reaches into the mammoth-sized bowl of popcorn.

It's *Skinny Pop*. I'm not going to gain back all the weight I worked so hard to lose just because my heart is broken.

Mom and I use a blanket to shield our eyes throughout the movie.

"How do people enjoy this?" she whispers.

"I don't know. This was a terrible choice."

"You can sleep in my bed tonight."

"I was planning on it."

We're watching a scene where the dumb, scantily-clad blond creeps around a shed. The high-pitched violins signal that it's time to pull up the blanket again. Just as the maniac with the chainsaw bursts onto the screen, the doorbell rings.

Mom and I shriek as popcorn flies everywhere.

"Jesus Christmas," Mom gasps. "Who's ringing our bell in the middle of a snow storm?"

"Don't open it! What if it's a man with a chainsaw?"

Mom rolls her eyes as she stands and unlocks the door. She peeks through the crack before swinging it wide open.

Jaxon.

It might as well be the guy with the chainsaw. My heart's hacked up all the same.

Still in his work suit with a black North Face over it, his hands are red from the cold. Flakes of snow sprinkle his dark hair, with a few caught in his eyelashes. He looks like he's freezing, as if he's been outside longer than his walk from the car to my porch.

"Are you guys all right in here?" he asks, stomping the snow off his boots. "I heard screaming."

Mom laughs. "We're watching *Texas Chainsaw Massacre*. The doorbell scared us."

Jaxon's eyes meet mine, and there's so much emotion behind them that I'm unable to move. *Why is he here?*

Mom clears her throat. "Well, I'm going to take a nice, long, bubble bath." She backs away and slinks up the stairs.

"Can I come in?" Jaxon asks.

"Sure." I look around at all the popcorn everywhere. I don't know what to say, what to do, what to think. My hands are shaking so I begin brushing the popcorn pieces off the cushion next to me.

Jaxon chuckles as he walks over and sits. "Scared you guys pretty good, huh?"

"Look, if you're here to fire me, just get it over with. I can take it." I sit up straight and brace myself.

His eyebrows collapse. "Why would I come to your house to fire you?"

"Why else would you be here?"

Jaxon reaches out for me, caressing my cheek with the back of his hand. "God, I've missed you."

My breath hitches. "So you're not going to fire me?"

"No. Becca told me everything."

"Everything?"

"She told me the truth about the ring. What you tried to do for my family. I came here straight from my parents' house."

"Your parents? Oh, no. Jaxon, what happened?"

He shakes his head, a smile tugging at his lips. "After what we've put you through, you're still worried about me and my family."

I shrug. "It's a genetic flaw."

He laughs and puts his hands around my waist, sliding me across the couch and onto his lap. "You are anything but flawed, Ms. Donahue."

I close my eyes and touch my forehead to his. "So what does this mean? You're here, the truth's out in the open ..."

"This means that I'm here to get you back. I'll do anything I can to make you say *yes*."

Butterflies swarm my stomach. "Well, if you recall, I'm partial to begging."

Jaxon pushes me off his lap. He lowers himself onto the floor, crunching popcorn under his knees, all the while wearing that delicious smirk on his face.

I bite my bottom lip to keep from smiling.

He takes my hands in his and looks into my eyes. "Please forgive me and my family for all the pain we've caused you. Please, Raegan. Say you'll be with me again. Say you still love me as much as I love you."

A laugh escapes me and I throw my arms around his neck. "That was good, Waters. I could get used to that."

Jaxon presses his lips to mine for a chaste kiss. "Is that a yes?"

"Yes to all of the above."

He dives on top of me, the rest of the popcorn spilling out of the bowl. Gripping my face, he kisses me, long and hard.

"I love you so much, Raegan."

"I love you too."

CHAPTER FORTY

Days Left Until Summer Break: 68
Jaxon

"*A*re you sure you want to do this?"

Raegan squeezes my hand. "Yes. I haven't changed my mind in the last seven seconds since you last asked me."

"I just want you to know that you don't have to do this for me."

"I'm doing this for us. They're your family, and we need to sort this out sooner or later. Your poor mother needs some peace."

I blow out a stream of air through my lips. "Okay. But the second you feel angry, or you want to leave, tell me."

"I won't get angry. I'm cool as a cucumber."

I lift my hand and turn the knob, stepping into my parents' house.

Mom greets us immediately. She flings her arms around Raegan. "Thank you so much for coming. It means the world to me. I'm so happy you two were able to work things out."

Raegan smiles. "I'm looking forward to putting all of this behind us."

Dad emerges from the kitchen. He nods at me, and I nod back. Raegan might be able to forgive him, but I'm not ready yet.

He reaches out and squeezes Raegan's shoulder. "I'm sorry I involved you in our family issue. I should've never put you in the middle like that. I hope you can forgive me."

Raegan covers his hand with hers. "Thank you for your apology. While I don't agree with what you did, I understand why you did it."

"You do?"

"You were trying to keep the peace between your children. I probably would've done the same thing."

Dad exhales and his shoulders drop. "Thank you for understanding. It's been difficult between my two boys. I wish it didn't have to be like this."

Josh steps into the living room, hands in his pockets. We all look at him, waiting for him to offer Raegan an apology like Dad.

He shrugs. "Sorry."

Anger courses through me. I open my mouth to say something, but Raegan's hand pats my shoulder. "I've got this," she says.

She walks toward Josh, a small smile on her sweet, innocent face. When she gets in front of him, her fist rockets toward his face. Mom gasps, and Josh rears back, pinching his nose as blood spills out of his nostrils. My jaw drops.

Raegan steps closer to him, pointing her finger in his face. "That wasn't for me."

"Then what the hell was that for?" he asks, backing away from her.

"*That* was for screwing around with Jaxon's ex."

I don't try to fight the smile that's spreading across my face. I pull Raegan to my side and plant a kiss on the top of her head. "I can't wait to see what you do to him for stealing the ring."

She smiles. "I'm not going to retaliate against him for the ring."

"You're not?" Josh and I ask at the same time.

"Everything that happened has led us to this point," she says, looking around the room. "Jaxon and I might not be together if Josh never stole the ring. It was a crazy roller coaster ride, but we're here. So I'd like to put all of this behind us now and start fresh. A clean slate."

Raegan walks over to my father and extends her hand. "It's nice to meet you, Mr. Waters. You and your wife have a lovely home."

Dad chuckles, shaking her hand. "Thank you, Raegan. It's a pleasure to meet the girl who captured my son's heart."

"Let's all have a seat at the table." Mom ushers us into the dining room. "Dinner's ready."

We take our seats and dig in.

It'll take me some time to forgive my father for conspiring against me, but I know I'll get there. As for Josh, who's sitting across from me with a bloody tissue shoved up his nose, I don't think things will ever be okay between us. Maybe he'll change. Maybe he won't.

Either way, I'll always have the memory of Raegan punching him.

I look at the beautiful woman beside me, who's icing her swollen hand.

God, I love this woman.

EPILOGUE

Two Years Later
Jaxon

"*H*appy Anniversary, baby."

Raegan clinks her glass against mine. "Happy Anniversary."

"Can you believe we're here? After everything we've been through."

Her eyebrow arches. "You mean after everything you put me through?"

I chuckle. "To be fair, it was a crazy coincidence that Nana's ring disappeared the same night I took you to my apartment."

"I'll give you that."

"And I get points for taking care of you while you threw up all night. With a raging hard-on, might I add."

"And they say chivalry is dead." Her eyes roll but she's smiling.

I slide my hand across the table and interlace our fingers. "I miss seeing you at work every day, like we used to."

"Me too. I hate that you had to transfer to a different school because of me."

"It's not because of you. It's because I want to be with you, for real … like out in public. We couldn't sneak around forever."

"I know, I know. But the sneaking around was fun those last few months."

"Yes. Yes, it was." My dick hardens at the memory of all the things we did in my old office at Roosevelt Elementary.

Before I get carried away, I chug the last of my water. *Focus, Waters.* It's showtime. I stand and button my jacket, making sure my tie is straight.

"Where are you going?" Raegan asks.

"Oh, did I forget to tell you? I'm the guest speaker tonight."

"Jaxon, why are you smirking like that?" She tugs on my arm. "What are you up to?"

I wink and place a kiss at the top of her head. Then I approach the stage, swiping the microphone off the stand.

"Good Evening, everyone. Thank you for coming out tonight to join me in celebration of our incredible teachers." I pause while everyone applauds, taking this time to search for Raegan's mother in the crowd.

She waves and gives me a thumbs-up, holding her phone above the crowd at the back of the room.

"Tonight is a special night. Every year, one teacher from each school is nominated by his or her colleagues to be the Teacher of the Year. To be nominated means that teacher has gone above and beyond the call of duty as a teacher. We have eight teachers with us tonight who've inspired and astounded us. Let's give a round of applause for these incredible teachers."

Another pause. This time, my gaze locks with Raegan's.

What are you up to, Waters? her eyes ask.

You're about to find out, I silently reply.

"Before we get started, I'd like to call a very special teacher up here with me. Raegan Donahue, please join me on stage."

Raegan's cheeks burn as friends and faculty cheer for her. Becca motions for Raegan's mother to take her seat up in the front of the room.

I clear my throat as Raegan walks toward me, and take her hand in mine.

"What is this?" she grits through a smile.

I lift the microphone. "Raegan Donahue, you are without a doubt the love of my life. They say everything happens for a reason, and I believe it. For the past three years, you've made me the happiest man in the world. Your beauty drew me to you, but it was your intelligent mind, your quick wit, and your larger-than-life heart that enraptured me. I can't imagine spending my life with anyone else. And that's why, in front of your family and friends, I'm asking you ..."

I drop down on one knee and open the blue velvet box that started this whole thing.

Raegan's hands fly to her mouth, her watery eyes wide.

"Raegan, will you let me love you forever and be my wife?"

The room is silent, awaiting her response. I took a chance proposing to Raegan with the ring that nearly ended us a few years ago, but it just felt right. So I trusted my gut. It has never steered me wrong.

After several painful seconds tick by, Raegan nods. "Yes," she whispers, tears streaming down her beautiful face. "Yes, of course I'll marry you!"

I spring to my feet and wrap my arms around her, spinning her in a circle while the room erupts in cheers.

She pulls my face to hers and lays a soft kiss on my lips. "You know, I wouldn't've said yes if you'd proposed with any other ring."

I laugh. "I couldn't picture you wearing anything else."

The ring thief might not have stolen the ring after all, but she did steal my heart.

The End

Want more from the Roosevelt Elementary gang? Read: Back to You

Chapter Forty-One

MORE FROM KRISTEN

The Collision Series Box Set with Bonus Epilogue
Collision: Book 1
Avoidance: Book 2, Sequel
The Other Brother: Book 3, Standalone
Fighting the Odds: Book 4, Standalone
Hating the Boss: Book 1, Standalone
Inevitable: Contemporary standalone
What's Left of Me: Contemporary standalone
Dear Santa: Holiday novella
Someone You Love: Contemporary standalone

Want to gain access to exclusive news & giveaways?
Sign up for my monthly newsletter!

Visit my website: https://kristengranata.com/
Instagram: https://www.instagram.com/kristen_granata/
Facebook: https://www.facebook.com/kristen.granata.16
Twitter: https://twitter.com/kristen_granata

Want to be part of my KREW?

Join Kristen's Reading Emotional Warriors
A Facebook group where we can discuss my books, books you're
reading, and where friends will remind you what a badass warrior
you are.

Love bookish shirts, mugs, & accessories?
Shop my book merch shop!

ACKNOWLEDGMENTS

First and foremost, thank you to my wife. Your support & encourage-ment on my writing journey keeps me going. I love you beyond life and I'm so lucky to have you as my partner. It's not easy dealing with me and my writing obsession, but you help me every step of the way & I appreciate that more than you'll ever know. Somehow, some way, I will get you that porch!

My cover designer & friend, Taylor – you are awesome! You make my ideas come to life. I'm so thankful for your help & your friendship.

To my "muses" who lent me their names for these characters: Becca, Sammi, Mary, Andrea, and Kerry, I love you ladies. Thank you for your ideas & feedback. I hope you laughed while seeing "your" characters in this book. Hopefully one day, we can all meet up for real drinks!

Dorthy, my bestie, thank you for allowing me to include your unforgettable pen-on-leg story. Now, it will be preserved within the pages of this book forever! Thank you for reading (and re-reading) every single one of my books, and for taking notes to tell me what you think.

To the readers, bloggers, & bookstagrammers: Your support means everything to me. Thank you for helping me get my books out there. You guys make me excited to write. I hope one day I can sign books for you at some big author event, and give you a big, awkward hug!

Made in the USA
Las Vegas, NV
03 January 2022

40252631R00125